ALIEN GENIE

ALIEN GENIE

JOHN FITZGERALD

authorHOUSE®

AuthorHouse™
1663 Liberty Drive
Bloomington, IN 47403
www.authorhouse.com
Phone: 1 (800) 839-8640

Published by AuthorHouse   07/11/2015

ISBN: 978-1-5049-2236-4 (sc)
ISBN: 978-1-5049-2235-7 (e)

Library of Congress Control Number: 2015911000

Print information available on the last page.

Michael Greiner was going hunting. He hadn't gone hunting in a couple of years simply because he had met this girl and had found other things to do with his time in the fall. But, the relationship had soured, and they went their separate ways. When the regular group of friends he had gone hunting with over the years had found out he was free again, they insisted he come this year. He had always enjoyed the week in the mountains, so he told them he would go this year.

Michael was in his thirties, single and living alone in his own house in a small town in northern New Jersey. He had a good job and was happy with his lot in life. Mike took a month's vacation from his job as a Postal Supervisor and was really looking forward to this hunting season.

The night before he was to leave for the mountains, he loaded his car and was settling down with a beer and his favorite tape, "Somewhere in time" when the phone rang.

"Hello"

"Hello Mike?"

"Yeah Phil, it's me."

"Just want to make sure you're coming up tomorrow."

"Of course I'm coming up, I got the booze like you asked, did you get the beer?"

"Yeah, Don and I picked up 10 cases of "Sam Adams" just like you wanted. And bob is bringing the food."

"Good, I get the feeling this is going to be one of the best hunting seasons we've ever had."

"Yeah, well it's going to be one of the drinkenest one's we've ever had."

"Sounds good to me Phil, see you in the morning and don't forget to bring money, I haven't had a good card game in a few year."

"Don't worry about anything Mike, all has been arranged, food and drink and there's only going to be four of us the first week, the others will be up this next Friday night."

"Good, I'm looking forward to seeing every one again."

"Okay, until tomorrow then, good night Mike."

"Yeah, good night my friend."

Mike hung up the phone, popped open the beer and sat back to enjoy his movie, at about eleven thirty he went to sleep. Mike thought to himself as he closed his eyes. "I get the feeling this is going to be one hell of exciting weekend."

In his wildest dreams, he could never guess just how right he was.

It was now about four in the morning and the alarm went off. Mike sat up on the edge of the bed holding his head. He looked at the clock and fell back down on the bed.

"What the hell am I doing up at this hour." "Oh well, it's only one week out of the year."

Mike got up, showered shaved and made some breakfast. Closed up the house, and asked his neighbors if they would look after things while he was gone. He lived in that kind of area, where you're next door neighbor was someone you could trust with your house and possessions.

Six o'clock found Mike on state hwy 17 heading west. He paced himself and kept within the speed limit of 55mph. It was a beautiful fall day and the entire week was supposed to be in the upper 50's; ideal weather. Mike got off at the Roscoe exit and headed inland. He arrived at the cabin at around 9:30, unloaded the car and put everything in the house. Unpacked and took his rifle outside along with the morning paper and a cup of coffee. He loved it up here and had really missed the last couple of years hunting. Mike sat back and started to read the funnies, his favorite part of the paper, when he heard three more cars coming up the road.

"Oh well." He thought, "All good things must come to an end."

The cars pulled up to the house and emptied.

"Hey Mike, good to see ya."

"Yeah, good to see you too Don."

"It's been to long between visits Mike." Bob said

"Yeah, tell me about it I've really missed this place."

"Well the next time you get yourself a girl, make sure she don't mind you going hunting." Phil added.

Every one put their stuff away and brought out their rifles and handguns, it was a kind of tradition to show off what you were going to hunt with this season.

Bob looked over at the rifle Mike was handling and said

"Where did you ever get that from?" He reached over and took the weapon from Mike.

"My neighbor gave it to me., he had it for years, I seen it a couple of times when I was in his house and I admired it." "So, just before he moved to Florida, he came over to the house."

"Sort of like a going away present in reverse."

"Man, this is old, look at this it says here on the receiver, "Springfield model 1898""

Don looked at the rifle and said

"Must be a 30 cal., right?" – "30/40 Cal. Made for this rifle and never again."

"Yeah, and I'm going to get me the biggest deer in the woods with it because I'm going to hunt on the top of the mountain." Mike said

"The top of the mountain?" "Are you nuts? No one has ever gone up there." Phil said as he reached for the weapon to give his opinion of it.

"Yeah." Bob added "It's just too hard to get to, you'll fall and get hurt, it's too steep a climb."

"Well I'm going to do it any way, I'm going to start out real early and I'll be the first one of us to hunt up there." "The way I figure it is there has to be an easy way up there, and I'm going to find it.

"Well, good luck, myself, I'm going to hunt the lower pines." Don said. All eyes looked over at Bob

Bob slowly stopped cleaning his rifle when he felt all the eyes on him.

"Yeah, yeah I know, and I still say I was robbed, never mind almost killed."

Everyone one started to laugh, it was a standing joke on Bob that he would never live down. It seems about 5 year ago that Bob came up hunting in a camouflaged outfit. Now according to state laws you can't hunt with a rifle wearing a camouflaged suit. You blend into the background to easily and can get killed by some hunter who thinks he sees a deer behind that moving bush. Well any way it seems Bob went into the lower pines to hunt that day. But because of the late card game and all the drinking the night before, he was still a little tipsy and fell asleep beneath a tall pine. And about 100 yards to his left there was another hunter sitting by this big rock and he didn't see Bob because of what Bob was wearing. So along comes this big 10 pointer and it's standing next to the tree Bob is sleeping under. Well, Bob awoke to a big bang and a deer falling at his feet. He rants and raves, arguing with this hunter about almost being killed. That noise attracted a game warden. The results, the other hunter got to keep the deer and Bob got a big fine for wearing a camouflaged outfit.

"You know I was robbed, I said it before and I'll say it again, I was robbed."

After the laughter stopped and everyone had cleaned their weapons and generally did everything that had to be done before setting out in the morning, everyone went inside and relaxed reading and watching TV before the evening meal and the big card game that would follow.

The next morning Bob was the first one up as usual. He started the coffee and the eggs and bacon which aroused everyone else. After breakfast was over and the dishes were put away, everyone started to get dressed.

"Well look at the deer hunter." Phil said pointing to Mike who was the first one dressed.

"I told you guys I was going to leave early to get to the top of the mountain."

"Yeah, well good luck, I hope you brought a whistle with you."

"Why would I need a whistle?"

"Well, after you fall from trying to climb up the mountain, and you're lying in deep brush at the bottom of the ravine, you'll have to blow the whistle so we can find you." Another round of laughter from all assembled

"Ha ha real funny, I'll see you guy's later." And Mike walked out the door

Mike had to do some steep climbing to get to the top, and it took him the better part of two hours to reach the summit. But when he finally got to the top and looked down to where he just came from he said

"Now I know why no one has ever hunted up here, Phew that was some climb, I got to rest a little."

Mike looked at the level he had reached. The plain before him was a level stretch of ground about 500 hundred yards wide and maybe 300 yards deep. He saw that the mountain continued to go up for what Looked like another mile to the far end of the field before him. Mike walked toward the end of the field where the incline started again and there in the wall he spotted a small indent, just big enough to protect someone from rain or snow. You could build a small fire and settle in for the night if you had to. He settled down and broke out the thermos of coffee he brought in his back pack along with several cookies and an orange.

"It's funny how a climb like that will use up everything you ate for breakfast." He said to himself.

Mike looked around; he had an excellent field of fire. He could see for at least 150 yards in front and to the sides. He thought to himself

"Boy, if the others could only see this place, maybe I'll talk them into coming up here tomorrow."

"This is the greatest spot I've ever seen around here."

The sun was just beginning to peek from around the thick cloud cover. It was going to be a beautiful day. He put the thermos away and threw the orange peels out into the grass. He couldn't believe the view he had from this spot. There was nothing in front of him except some grass that was about a foot high. Mike sat back and cradled the rifle. He watched the sun work its way around the tall dark gray clouds. The clouds had started to dissipate leaving the sun by its self and a few of the real bright stars that were competing with the sun for his attention. Mike sat there for another 30 minutes just listening to the sounds of the birds and the rustling of the branches of the trees. He couldn't believe how beautiful this spot was. About four clicks to the west of the sun Mike saw a star sitting on the horizon. It was a bright star and Mike figured it was Venus.

"Good morning Venus, you are beautiful as usual."

He kept his eyes moving looking to the edge of the forest. You usually see the Doe come out of the forest first, and then the buck emerges. As if he said,

"Go on, you go out first to see if the coast is clear."

But there was nothing yet. He was sitting in this spot for about 45 minutes and all he saw so far were rabbits and raccoons.

"That's all right I've got all day." He thought to himself "Times on my side."

It was starting to get cool; he could see more clouds moving in from the west

"I guess it's going to be cooler than the weather man thought, goes to show you what they know." He changed his position to make himself a little more comfortable. Mike noticed the star, it seemed to be getting larger, but its position in the sky remained the same. Mike had a scope mounted on the rifle in a way that it wouldn't tap into the metal of the weapon and take from its value. He picked up the weapon and pointed it at the star to get a better look.

"Yeah, that's Venus alright." "Must be the altitude, thinner air."

Mike put the rifle down and picked up the binoculars he brought and started to scan the edges of the forest. Another ten minutes past and Mike is looking at the star again.

"That can't be Venus, it's getting bigger." He said to no one. He picked up the rifle and looked at the light through the scope.

"Nope, that's no plane." Just then his eye caught movement at the edge of the forest, to his left front.

"Hot damn a deer." Mike said, "Shit it's a buck."

Mike saw the biggest deer he had seen in years coming out of the forest and it had at least twelve points. His hand started to shake as he swung the rifle from the light to the deer. In his excitement, he fired to fast and missed the deer by inches. The round hit the tree just in front of the animal. No time for a second shot the target vanished.

"Shit, I fired to quickly, shit." Mike was too busy cursing himself to notice the light had changed its direction and was coming right at him. When he did notice, he said

"What the." He again looked through the scope. The light was getting bigger and closer and brighter. He didn't know what to do, at first, he thought it was a meteor or a comet or a plane or he didn't know what to think. His mind was running wild and he couldn't figure any place to run. This thing was getting too close. Mike was scared. All of a sudden the light stopped. It came to a stop in the clearing about 50 yards in front of him. It was so bright it out shone the sun. When he collected his wits, the first thing to come into his mind was UFO. Mike looked around for some place to run when it spoke to him.

"You creature." Mike stopped breathing. He thought he heard something, but he wasn't sure.

"You creature, come here, now" There it was again, like someone talking in his head. "Come closer, you won't be hurt; no harm will come to you."

Mike looked around; he didn't know what to do. He figured he was dreaming.

"You with the weapon, come closer, NOW." He jumped. He wondered if anyone else could see or hear this thing. He must be dreaming. Mike sat down and rubbed his eyes.

"Maybe if I rub my eyes this thing will go away." Now he felt a strange force kind of grab him and force him to stand. He started to walk towards the light. He didn't want to, but he was heading towards the light like it or not.

Mike was getting closer to this light; he wanted to get the hell out of here but couldn't go in any other direction except straight ahead. He thought to himself.

"Something is very wrong here, and I'm getting a little worried."

When he got within ten yards of the light, Mike stopped. Again he heard the voice.

"I have come a great distance to meet with you." "How are you called?"

This was all in his head, and Mike wasn't sure he wasn't a little hung over from last night. Although he didn't remember drinking too much at all.

"I've got to be dreaming." Mike thought to himself

"HOW ARE YOU CALLED?" Mikes head rocked back, if that had been a spoken question; it would have broken his eardrums.

"Who wants to know?" "Or should I ask, what wants to know?"

"DO NOT MOCK ME, COSMIC SLIME; ANSWER ME, HOW ARE YOU CALLED?"

Again his head rocked back.

"What the fuck are you shouting about? I'm right here; I'm not a mile away." Mike figured as long as it seems he couldn't control his present situation, he had nothing to lose in talking back to this, this, whatever it was. All of a sudden the light was getting dimmer and dimmer. Then standing before him was this thing. Mike figured it was the alien that had been speaking to him in his mind. And he was convinced that if he could just move his feet, he would be out of here in a flash.

"Welcome to earth, do you want me to take you to my leader?" Mike chuckled to himself.

Mike found himself lying on his back about ten feet from where he remembered he was standing a second ago, and he hurt all over.

"I told you not to mock me, I don't have long to go and your atmosphere is making me sick."

"There is something I must give to you, and I don't have much time left." Mike tried to stand up, but couldn't remain standing and fell to his knees.

"What the fuck happened?" He thought to himself.

"Come closer NOW." Again the shouting in his head

Mike again got to his feet and staggered closer to this creature, and again thought "If I could run, I'd be far away from here real quick." Now he heard the voice in his head speak again, but to someone or something else. "Here is your creature, I have fulfilled my part of the bargain, now send me home."

All of a sudden there was another light; it just appeared next to the alien. When the light went out, what appeared looked to Mike like a large TV remote control unit just floating in the air. Again the alien spoke to Mike.

"I hope you enjoy what I am going to give to you."

"Use it wisely, this that I give you is your slave, it will do anything you ask it to do."

"But be very careful what it is you ask for Earthman, be very careful." Now Mike heard another voice.

"He will do, you have done well, now go and rest." "You have a lot of sins to atone for."

"You are not my judge, so do not tell me what I must do, just send me home as your part of the bargain."

"One more thing Earthman, when it is your time to go to your ancestors, you must pass this gift I give you on to another being in another galaxy." "Do you understand?"

Mike stood there, really not believing this was happening.

"DO YOU UNDERSTAND WHAT I HAVE TOLD YOU EARTHMAN?"

For the third time his head rocked back.

"Stop shouting you son of bitch, you're hurting my neck." Mike yelled "And yes I understand, when I die I have to give this to someone else." Now the alien turned to the control unit.

"I am sorry I have picked such a low form of life for you."

"It is alright, he will learn, now go to your rest." Before Mikes eyes the first alien disappeared

Mike stood there looking at this control unit and then it spoke to him and started to come closer.

"Don't be afraid, this well not hurt you." "We will be together for the rest of your life, and I have to get to know your mind." Mike couldn't move yet and this thing was getting closer to his head. Now he started to panic again, this thing was moving at him at eye level, and before he could think of anything else it had moved through his head, he could almost feel it going through.

Now the thing was in front of him again and said

"Now Michael, what would you like to do?" Mike was sitting on the ground holding his head.

"What happened?" "Was I dreaming, or did I just hear a space command unit talk to me."

Mike looked around, and for a minute he was disoriented. He remembered sitting in the little hole in the side of the wall and looking at the light getting bigger, and then there was the deer.

"Yeah, now I remember, I missed that big buck." "But what the hell am I doing out here?"

"You came out to receive me Michael." Mike was rubbing his head because of the sudden strange feeling that came over him. When he heard the voice, he froze for a second and then looked up to see this strange alien thing floating in the air in front of him.

"Oh yeah, now I remember, you came out of that light with that, that creature."

"Yes Michael, I was brought here and handed over to you as part of the bargain I made with what you call the alien creature."

"Look before we go any further, do you mind explaining to me just what the hell is going on here?"

"Yes Michael, I am what you would call a machine, a very advanced machine." "Far more advanced than anything your world could produce."

"I was sent out by those that made me to travel to alien worlds and seek out a creature like yourself."

"And when I find one I am to stay with that creature until its life in this dimension is over."

"Then I will be given over to another creature on another world to continue my mission."

Mike was looking at this alien machine and listening to what it was saying and still not believing this wasn't part of some hangover from the night before.

"And what if I may ask, is your mission."

"On the world I come from, all work is done by thought" "The people that sent me out on this mission are the oldest race of beings in this universe." "My mission was one of searching for entertainment."

"Entertainment?"

"Yes Michael, I was to find an alien life form and unite with it for the rest of its life." "Then once united with it, I transmit back to the world I came from everything the life form would do, its entire life until the end of its life in this universe."

Mike thought for a moment and then said

"You mean the people who sent you out would watch what you sent back and that was to them, entertainment?"

"Yes Michael, every thought, every word every action." "This to them was entertainment."

"You would manipulate the creature for their entertainment?"

"No Michael, I do not command, I obey, I grant wishes I do as I am asked as I am commanded."

"And the race that sent you just sits back and watches what goes on."

"Yes, that is right." "You see Michael, the race that sent me out is the oldest race in this dimension."

"They had progressed to a point where everything was done by thought, they had done everything seen everything and been everywhere." "They had reached a point where life was boring." "And then they came up with the idea of watching other races on other worlds and seeing how they lived."

"Sort of like a travel show, watch before you go there sort of thing."

"Yes Michael, only I can make things happen, I can do whatever you wish me to do."

"Are you going to be hanging in the air in front of me for the rest of my life?"

Mike stopped and thought for a minute. He couldn't believe what was happening, was this real?

Or was this a dream. It couldn't be a dream, it was too real.

"No Michael, before I take my place in your life, we have to make an agreement."

"What kind of an agreement?"

"Did you understand what you were told by the alien?"

"You mean about my giving you to another life form before I die?"

"Yes, do you understand what is required of you?"

Mike was thinking how he could get rid of this thing if he ever got tired of it.

"There is no way you can rid yourself of me before your time in this dimension is over Michael."

"How did you know what I was thinking?"

"I united with your mind Michael, did you forget?" "I know your thoughts."

"Oh yeah, I forgot." "As to your question, yes I understand, but space travel is not one of my better talents." "Don't worry about anything Michael, I can do anything you want me to do."

"Okay, I'm convinced, now, about you hanging in the air." And with that said the alien machine vanished.

Mike looked around to see where the thing had gone. "Where are you now?"

"Somewhere above you, but don't bother looking up, you will not see me."

"But remember always, Michael, I am with you until the end."

"If you don't mind I'd like to get back to hunting, watching you come in my scope made me miss a large buck."

"Would you like another shot at this animal you missed?"

"Boy would I. That had to be one large buck, I bet he was at least a ten pointer."

Mike was walking back to the little cave that he had been sitting in when all this happened, when he picked up movement out of the corner of his eye.

"There he is again." Mike was whispering. He picked up his rifle and looked through the scope. He put the cross hairs on the heart and was slowly pulling the trigger. Then He stopped,

"There's something wrong here." He said lowering the rifle

"There is the animal you were aiming at Michael, go ahead and kill it, that's what you want isn't it?"

"Well yeah, but not exactly, I mean this looks like he's frozen in that position."

"He is."

"Well that's not fair, I can't just shoot him like that."

"Why not Michael?"

"Well there's no sport in that, I mean I could walk up to it and butt stroke it in the head, that's no fun."

"But you are hunting an animal that can't really hurt you, it poses no threat to you in any way."

"And you are hunting it with a large caliber weapon that doesn't give it any kind of a chance."

"Yeah, so?"

"If you are looking for fairness in this sport, as you call it, why not hunt an animal that can hunt you back?"

"We have the black bear that can defend itself."

"Can it really Michael."

"The bear you refer to is a slow lumbering beast that would rather leave you alone and run away than hunt you." Mike smiled and said

"You never saw a black bear run down and kill a deer, did you, let me tell you their fast."

"Yes Michael, it can run down and kill a deer." "But a deer isn't armed with a weapon that can kill at great distances."

"I mean an animal like this." And before Mike could replay again he caught movement to his left. He turned in the direction of the movement and spotted that resembled the white tail deer he was used to seeing in the woods. But they're the resemblance ended. It had antlers like an elk. But when the beast caught Mikes smell and turned in his direction, it stood up on its hind legs to reveal two front arms that ended in two clawed hands that were almost human. As he watched the beast, the mouth opened to expose fangs and two rows of teeth that were meant to kill and tear flesh. All of a sudden the thing let out a roar that made Mike take a couple of steps back. Taken completely by surprise, Mike didn't know exactly what to do.

"What the fuck is that."

"That Michael is called a Throot on its home world which is in a galaxy a thousand light years from here." As Mike was listening to the alien, the beast started to charge. Almost in a complete panic, Mike picked up his rifle and fired a shot in the direction of the horror that was coming at him. At the same time, he stepped back and fell over a rock, landing heavily, and hit his right elbow on a rock. He cried out in pain. Looking up, Mike saw the beast make a leap into the air and was coming down on top of him when it vanished in mid leap. Grabbing his right elbow Mike said.

"Ow, I think I broke my arm." "And what the fuck was that all about?" Mike started to feel heat in the broken joint.

"Did you bring that thing here to kill me or to scare the shit out of me, which it did."

No Michael, I didn't bring it here to kill you."

"I thought you would enjoy the chance to hunt something that could hunt you in return."

"Oh you did, did you."

"Yes Michael that is the way hunters in primitive societies prove their manhood."

"Oh really, well let me tell you something." Mike stood up feeling his now healed elbow and looking around for something to talk to and brushing the dirt off of himself. Picking up his rifle he started to walk back to the cave.

"In case you haven't noticed, we are a highly advanced world." Feeling his elbow again he continued

"We don't hunt to prove our manhood, at least not in this country."

"As we approached your world, I had time to scan it."

"Michael, your world is by far one of the most primitive societies I've had to work with." Mike continued to walk back to the cave. When he reached it he looked back to the spot where the light appeared scratched his head and settled down for some more hunting. Looking up in the air he asked.

"Are you real or is this some kind of dream?"

"I am real Michael." Mike looked at his watch, 0945.

"Good." He thought "I can still get in a full days hunting." With that thought in his head he fell asleep.

He woke up with a jolt. It was completely dark; the only light came from the Milky Way that was visible in all its glory.

"What the––what happened?" Mike started to feel around for the backpack he brought with him. When he found it he fumbled through it for the flashlight. When he found it he looked at his watch

"Six thirty, how the hell did I sleep so long?"

"This is a normal reaction to my joining with your mind."

"Who said that?" Mike pointed the flashlight in several directions looking for the source of the voice. Then he remembered.

"It wasn't a dream, was it?"

"No Michael, it was no dream, I will be with you until you pass from this dimension."

"You mean I don't get three wishes and you leave?"

"No Michael, I am not a genie, you remember how I arrived on your world?" "I am with you for the rest of your life."

"Whatever you say, but right now I'd like to get back to the cabin, the guys will be worried and start to look for me."

"Do you wish to return to the cabin now?"

"Yeah now would be nice." And with that said, Mike started to get up and start the long walk back.

As he stood up he found himself standing at the front door to the cabin.

"You don't fool around do you?"

"You wanted to return, so here you are." He heard voices behind him moving up the hill.

"Maybe we should go straight to the top, that's where he was going this morning, maybe we'll meet him coming down."

"Yeah, maybe."

"Hey guys, I'm over here." Mike yelled.

"Mike, Mike is that you? Where are you?"

"I'm over here by the cabin." Now the voices were getting closer, they were coming back.

Don was the first to reach him. "Where the hell were you."

"We've been worried about you."

"Yeah, we figured you shot the biggest deer in the woods and had trouble dragging it back." Phil added.

"I figured you met a beautiful girl up there and found something else to do beside hunt."

"Well let's go inside, I'm starving and I'll tell you all about it."

The hunters, back inside the cabin, were putting their gear away. Don went over to the fridge and got a beer. Phil and Bob busied themselves washing and putting away the supper dishes. After getting out of his hunting clothes, Mike was over by the wood burning stove in the kitchen getting warm.

"Okay, start at the beginning, what does she look like?" Don asked

"Yeah, and why didn't you bring her back here so we can all meet her?" Bob added. And everyone laughed.

"No, you got it all wrong, there was no girl, at least I don't think it's a girl." Mike was going over in his mind the events of the day and some of his thoughts were coming out as words.

"What do you mean by that", Don asked. Don was the closest friend Mike had in the group. He knew Mike the longest and they had been friends since they were children. Mike realized what he had said and tried to take it back what had slipped out.

"Are you still here?" Mike asked looking up at the ceiling. Don putting the beer to his lips, looked at the ceiling with Mike. Phil answered the question thinking it was directed at him.

"Of course we're still here, what kind of a question is that." In his head Mike heard the answer he had hoped to hear.

"Yes Michael, I'm still hear."

"Good, I keep thinking I'm going crazy." Bob and Phil turned to look at Don. They all glanced at Mike and again at each other and shrugged their shoulders.

Bob asked Mike what the three of them were thinking.

"Are you Okay Mike?" "Do you want to tell us what's the matter?"

"Look I don't think you guys are going to believe me when I tell you what happened to me up there."

"Well why don't you let us decide that, go ahead we're all ears." Phil added

"Okay, here goes."

"You know I went up to the top of the mountain this morning?"

"Well that's where you said you were going anyway." Don said smiling at his friend.

Mike picked up a can of beer and took a long swallow.

"I was sitting in this small depression in the wall, it's almost a cave, but not quite." "It's just big enough to keep you dry when it rains."

"I don't know how long I was sitting there, it's a beautiful place, you should all go up there and check it out."

"Yeah, yeah, we'll go up there tomorrow, never mind the view, just tell us what happened."

"Okay, ok, anyway I was sitting there looking at the stars when I noticed this one star getting closer and closer." "I couldn't believe my eyes, at first I thought it was a plane or a meteorite or something."

"I was looking at it through my scope when I see this buck step out of the forest."

"I was caught off guard, and fired too quickly." "I missed the ten pointer."

"Yeah, yeah you missed the deer and then the girl walks by right?"

"I keep telling you there was no girl." Phil popped open another beer and said

"Look there had to be a girl, what else would keep you out there all day."

"Well, after I fired the shot, I noticed that the star or whatever I was watching, changed direction an started to come right at me." Mike continued to relate the events of that morning's encounter with the alien, by the time he finished, two more six packs had been started.

"So what you're saying is now you have this alien machine inside your head? Bob asked leaning over the table and looking into Mike's eyes like he was trying to see the alien. Mike pushed Bob away and stood up.

"There's one more thing I didn't tell you." Phil walked over to Mike and put his arm around his shoulder. "I knew the girl would come up sooner or later." "Was she a blonde?"

"I know Don added, you met that ditzy dame from TV, Kelly Bundy." The three of them laughed.

"No, that's when this alien asks me if I would like to hunt something that could hunt me back."

"What do you mean, the forest is full of bear, I avoided two my self today." Phil said

"I said we have black bear and they can hunt us for food."

"So what happened next." Phil was getting caught up in the story.

"Well before I could say anything else, I see this strange animal, it was at least twice the size of the largest deer I've ever seen." "And it had antlers like an elk, but when it stood up to reach the lower branches of the tree it was under."

"It was then that I saw the claws."

"It had claws?" Don asked

"Yeah, and then it caught scent of me."

"What do you mean it caught scent of you."

"It turned its head in my direction and started to sniff the air, when it saw me it let out this horrible Screech like roar and charged me." Mikes friends sitting around the table an listening to this story looked at each other and then Don spoke.

"You expect us to swallow all this shit you're shoveling at us?"

"Yeah, I heard some whoppers, but aliens in your head and animals only Edgar Rice Burroughs could come up with, come on you can do better than that." Bob looked at Mike and said.

"I'd like to get a shot at that animal myself."

"Come to think of it, it would be a change of pace, so to speak." Phil added.

In Mikes head the alien spoke.

"If you want Michael, I can put the Throot back in the woods for you friends?" Mike was thinking.

"Look, if you guys want proof of what I'm telling you let me know."

"Yeah, let's see this alien you're talking about." Don said

"No I don't mean the alien, I was thinking along the line of the beast I saw."

The three other hunters looked at each other. Don poured each of them two fingers of Irish whiskey.

Mike looked his old friend right in the eye and said

"You bet I'm serious, I've always wondered how many of you big, brave hunters would be up here in the forest if there was something in the woods that could hunt and kill you."

Again the three hunters looked at each other, Phil spoke up.

"Okay, in that case, we'll go hunting together tomorrow."

"So be it, now if you'll excuse me, something has come up and I've got to leave."

Don looked at his friend.

"You're going home already?" "Tonight, right now?"

"Yeah, and I want you guys to call me tomorrow night after you come back in and let me know how things went." Mike walked around the table an headed for his room.

Bob moved to block Mike and said.

"Come on Mike, hang around for a couple a days, don't leave now, look outside, since we've come in its started to snow." They all went to the window and looked out. The snow had been coming down pretty steadily and there was a fine coat of snow covering the ground. Phil spoke up.

"Yeah, come on Mike hang around awhile, we're only kidding you."

"Phil, it's nothing personal, but something has come up and I've got to go." Mike opened the door to his room, entered and closed the door.

He stood there and looking up to the ceiling said.

"Are you still here?"

"Yes Michael, I'm still here, do you want to return to your home?"

"Yeah, right now and take the car also, that should make them think twice." Before he finished the sentence, he was standing in his living room.

Don and Phil were sitting around the table; Bob was just coming out of the bathroom. He approached the table, as he was zippering up his pants.

"You guys don't believe all that crap do you?" he asked.

"Of course not." Phil said

"But he had us going there for awhile with that beast stuff." Bob popped open another beer and said.

"You know, I'd love to get a shot at that thing."

"But things like that only exist in books, not in real life." Don walked over to Mike's room and knocked on the door.

"Hey Mike, can I come in for a minute?"

"What's up Don?" Bob asked.

"I want to ask him about next weekend"

"Shit, he'll be out in a minute, ask him then." Phil said.

"I don't know about that." Don said

"I've known Mike a long time and I can tell when he's pulling my leg."

"There was something in his eyes when he was talking, and I think he's telling us the truth."

"Oh come on now, you can't really believe what he said is the truth do you?" Bob asked

Don opened the door to Mike's room and it was empty.

"If it's not the truth, where is he?" Don said, opening the door wide and turning on the light. The others came over and looked into the room.

"Where the hell did he go, hey Mike." Phil yelled into the room, even though there was no place to hide.

"Hey look, the car's gone also." Bob said pulling the curtain open and looking out into the night.

"How the hell did he get out of the house without us seeing him?" Phil asked.

"I don't know how he did that." Don added. "But tomorrow, I'm going to be extremely careful when I go out into the woods." He looked at the others and said again.

"Very, very careful."

Michael stood in his living room and looked up at the ceiling.

"Man you don't fool around do you?"

"I have picked up a saying from your mind Michael, your wish is my command."

"Yeah, I'm beginning to like this arrangement."

"What would you like to do next Michael?"

"I'm not sure, let me sleep on it for awhile."

After a good night's sleep and a hardy breakfast, Mike walked over to the bookshelf and picked up one of his favorite books, the complete Valley of the Kings. He sat down in the armchair that was next to the big window in the living room and opened to the chapter on the tomb of King Tut.(Just before Mike started to read, a thought popped into his head.

"Sue, I was just thinking. My friends should be out in the woods by now hunting that beast you put there." "Yes Michael, I know what you want. And the Throot is back on its world.

I took it out while you were sleeping." "But how did you do that before I asked you to?"

"Remember Michael, I'm in you're mind, you asked me in you're dreams."

"Oh good, I really didn't want them or anybody else that came across that thing to get hurt.")

Reading several paragraphs and putting his head back, he closed his eyes and said.

"Now this is what I have in mind."

"I know what you have in mind Michael."

"Oh yeah, I forgot, you know what I'm thinking."

"Last night while you slept I completed the union with your mind."

"I have given you a deeper understanding of my abilities and there shouldn't be any more doubts in your mind as to what I can do." Mike closed the book for a minute and put his mind to thinking of what he was just told. After a minute or so he looked up at the ceiling and said.

"Yes, I understand now, I can see what happened yesterday and it all makes sense now."

"Good Michael, now we can proceed, what would you like to do next?"

"Well you know my friend, I have this thing about ancient Egypt."

Mike had always wished he could just pop back into time and visit Egypt in its glorious past, just walk around among the people and take a couple of pictures. Just see what went on in everyday life.

So after a day of planning, he had gone to the mall and stopped at the "Outdoors" store where he ran up his MasterCard account to the tune of $475.00, Mike was ready for the first trip back in time. He figured he could make a living taking scientists back in time and letting them study whatever they wanted to. But first, he would have to prove to them that he could do what he said he could. And so he planned the first trip to get some proof. Mike figured the best place to start would be the tomb of Tutankhamen,

"Are you ready Michael?"

"Yeah, I'm as ready as I'll ever be."

"Now exactly where are you going to put me?"

"You want to be put close to the tomb of this ancient king."

"You will be within 10 yards of and facing the tomb, you will be able to find it without any trouble."

"And remember Michael, I will always be with you, don't be afraid of anything."

When he first landed in the valley, he looked around quickly an returned. The sensations that he experienced in that brief first moment almost shorted out his brain.

"Wow, that was fantastic." Mike stood there panting and sweating, he was excited, overwhelmed, stunned. His emotions were running wild. Looking around for someone to talk to he again looked up and said.

"That was fantastic."

"You were there only 30 seconds Michael, you must not be afraid."

"Yeah, well that's easy for you to say, but I was there all alone, in a potentially dangerous situation, you bet your transistors I was afraid."

"I don't have any transistors Michael, you will not be in any danger."

"Look, I'm the one who's there, alone without anybody who can speak my language."

"I would feel better if I had a company of Marines with me, at least I could see them."

"Would you like a company of Marines with you Michael?"

"Very funny." Mike was shaking a little bit from his brief encounter with the past. He looked at the ceiling and said.

"Let's do it again."

"Do you wish to return to the same place?"

"Yeah, just remember where you put me, I don't want to be stranded 3500 years in the past."

"And don't get lost."

"I will be with you."

The words of the alien were still ringing in his ears when he found himself standing in the same spot he had left only minutes before. He looked up at the sky, there was still about an hour of sun left before it dipped below the rim of the canyon. He had to find himself a place to wait; it wouldn't be long before the first of the robbers appeared. The alien did a little checking on the history of ancient Egypt, and seems to know all there is to know about it. And this is the date, according to the alien, that the first break-in happened. Mike wanted to be here for the event, he figured it was the ideal opportunity to get some of the treasure that was taken from the tomb. Treasures that were know to have been in the tomb but were stolen by thieves. Items that if he took to any museum, they would know what they were. And he would have positive proof of his ability to travel back in time.

Mike was wearing the black ninja suit that he had purchased just for this occasion, and already he was regretting not taking into consideration the fact that Egypt was a very hot country. The black suit was absorbing heat very fast. But he was here and going to stay this time. He also brought with him a six-battery flashlight, and one of those lights that fits on your head so you can have light while you work with both hands. He had a co2 BB pistol stuck in his belt, and for the hell of it he brought along one of those compressed air horn cans, he figured it would come in handy for something.

He looked for the entrance to the tomb, but couldn't find anything that pointed to it. He knew the location from the book he had and the alien had given him the exact spot. Now he looked around for a spot to sit and wait for the robbers to arrive. He had to find a spot that wasn't too far away, but yet he could kind of blend in with. That's why he wore the black ninja suit. He figured if he sat real still, no one would see him in the dark. He walked up this hill that was behind him, there was a rock about sixty feet up, Mike climbed the incline an sat down next to the rock to wait. The sun was just slipping behind the rim the canyon. He didn't know how many men to expect, but he figured it would take about 5 or 6 men to dig up the tomb break into it and take out what they wanted and then leave before sunrise.

Mike made himself comfortable and sat back. With the sun down it was starting to get cool. There was a slight breeze coming from the direction of the Nile and it carried with it the aroma of a cooking fire from the other side of the river. He sat there with the pistol in one hand and the horn in the other. About 30 minutes had passed when he thought he heard a noise. Straining to hear it again, he leaned forward to get closer to the noise. There, he heard it again. With the sun going down, the stars were coming out, the canyon was quite. Mike looked in the direction of the river, and picked up the faint glow of a torch. Someone was coming. He tried to blend into the hillside a little more, he was beginning to get scared, then the voice inside of his head repeated the often-heard phrase. "Do not be afraid, I am here."

That gave him a little comfort, but not much. Now he could hear voices. Whoever were coming didn't care if anyone heard them or not.

"I guess there's more people in on this than I thought." Whoever were coming knew the date and time the guards would come around. Apparently this wasn't one of their inspection days. As the torches got closer, he could count 4 men. They were carrying tools that would be used to dig up the tomb.

When they arrived at the site of the tomb, they all started to dig. They knew exactly were the tomb was, not looking around an guessing, they knew just were to start to dig. Mike thought to himself.

"Boy this really sucks, The temple priests go to all this trouble to bury their king, thinking he will be safe for eternity, an members of the burial party come back at night and dig him up" not only that, but the guards are probably in on it also. It didn't take them long to dig down to the sealed door to the tomb; the feat was accomplished in about an hour. They stopped for a break and one of them climbed out and walked up the hill and stopped about 40 feet up. Mike figured this one was the lookout. He listened and thought he heard the others break through the first wall. He waited not wanting to scare them away before they got into the treasure. Another 15 minutes passed and Mike made his move. Standing up, he started down the hill slowly, the light from the stars gave him more light then he expected. He was almost down to the valley floor when he slipped. The lookout on the opposite hill heard the noise. He stood up and looked in Mike's direction. Mike figured with the element of surprise gone, he might as well go for broke.

Putting the air horn in his waist band pouch, Mike turned on the light on his head and started to run down the hill. By the time he had reached the bottom and started up the other side he had the flashlight on also. The guard on the side of the hill couldn't believe his eyes. All he saw was this shadowy figure and two small stars coming at him. He started to back up the hill and run, he was mumbling a prayer his mother taught him to say when he thought he was going to die. It was supposed to bring you right into paradise. He started to scream, but this was not the pre-arranged signal the others were expecting.

When the three men in the tomb heard his panicked scream they knew something was very wrong. As Mike got closer to the poor peasant who was trying to escape this demon, the man's bowls gave out and he fainted. Mike now turned to the three in the tomb. He had to get to them before they could run away. As he approached the steps leading down into the tomb, Mike heard the panic that had taken over. The thieves inside the tomb knew something was very wrong. They figured the guards from the necropolis had arrived unexpectedly and they were caught robbing pharaoh's tomb. And the punishment for that was death.

Mike got to the top of the stair leading into the tomb before those inside could climb out. He stood there panting heavily. The three thieves inside stopped and looked up at this figure dressed in black and they knew some demon from the nether world had come to get them. Standing at the top looking the thieves in the face, Mike hesitated. He was thinking to himself.

"I hate tomb robbers, I'm going to teach these three a lesson they will never forget." He reached into the pouch hanging on his waist and took out the air horn. He pointed it at the quivering trio in the tomb and gave a blast. Now not since the beginning of time had anybody heard an air horn. The sound of the horn made dust fall from the ceiling and walls in the tomb, the three men at the bottom of the steps fainted. The peaceful tranquility of the valley and surrounding hills was shattered. People in the small village across the Nile upon hearing this terrible noise fell to their knees. Surely the gods had discovered the four men from their tiny village, and soon would come to take revenge on their families.

Mike quickly descended into the tomb. He wanted to get this over with as quickly as possible. He came upon an eerie scene. The light from the fallen touches lying by the second wall looked like an entrance into hell. The hair on the back of Mike's neck was standing on end. He quickly searched with his flashlight and found three cloth bundles the thieves were going to take with them. Moving over to them, Mike looked through them and picked out the objects he thought he could use. He was thoroughly engrossed in what he was doing and had forgotten about the fainted thieves. When he was finished, Mike stood up and turned around to find the men facing him. They were lying prone with their arms outstretched. The smell of human excrement was drifting towards him. He looked at the thieves and said.

"How dare you disturb the sleep of Pharaoh." Then he realized they couldn't understand him. Again the voice in his head came to him.

"Would you like them to understand you?"

"Yes, I forgot they couldn't." He repeated what he had said before. The men before him just started to cry and mumble.

"I can't understand them."

"Would you like to understand them Michael?"

"Yes, I thought we had arranged that."

"You said you wanted them to understand you."

"Yeah, but I thought, never mind, we'll talk about this later." Again he spoke to the three men.

"Why have you desecrated pharaoh's tomb." There was no response.

"ANSWER ME!" If the three men could have gotten closer to the ground, they would have. Mike walked over to the closest one and kicked him in the side.

"ANSWER ME DOG, WHY DID YOU BREAK INTO PHARAOHS TOMB?"

"Forgive us great one, we are humble peasants and only intended to take a few trinkets to help us feed our little ones who are hungry."

"A FEW TRINKETS, NOW YOU NOT ONLY LIE TO ME, YOU INSULT MY INTELLIGENCE."

"GET UP ON YOUR FEET." The thieves stood up. And facing this terror from the nether world, they started to shake more. The waste from their emptied bowls running down their legs an falling on the floor.

"I have a weakness for humans, that is why the gods sent me, if they had sent another you would be dead by now."

"The gods have been restored to their proper places and are once again worshiped by the people"

Mike walked around the three shivering thieves.

"Long have the gods watched and taken note of those who desecrated the tombs of Osiris."

"Waiting for them to come to the scales with their hearts."

"And then they take their revenge on them."

"They are handed over to the eater of souls." The thieves looked at each other and fell again to their knees.

"I have been sent to make an example of you before all of Kemit." Mike was asking the alien to have a man's voice speak from out of the tomb, make believe it was the dead pharaoh.

"Okay Michael."

"I will bring you to the temple of Osiris and before all of the people I will torture you" now the thieves began to cry.

"Save your tears for the torture, you will shed many more before you die." All of a sudden a voice came out of the tomb.

"Wait, have mercy on them, as I loved them in life, I love all my people in death." Mike turned an dropped to his knees, bowing in the direction of Tuts sarcophagus. The three men looked again at each other and bowed lower if it were possible. They believed they were hearing the voice of the god Osiris.

"I hear and obey great one." Mike spoke as if he were talking to the god himself. He got up an turned to the men on the floor.

"Arise, you have been saved by the infinite mercy of the god Osiris."

"Return to your village and tell all the people that the gods are watching and will punish all who enter here." The three men stood up and crying tears of relief, bowing to Mike, they started to walk backwards up the staircase. Mike moved towards them and said.

"Go, and do not return, for the next time you may not get away so easily. He reached into his pouch and brought out the air horn and reached for the BB gun in his belt.

"Go, what are you waiting for." He let loose with a blast of the air horn, the three men practically flew up the stairs. Mike was right behind them firing at them with the gun. They ran with long blasts of the air horn following them.

"Poor devils, I hate myself for scaring them like that." Mike went down into the tomb and retrieved the cloth sack with the treasure he was taking. And looking up at the ceiling said.

"Okay my friend, take me home." By the time he finished speaking, he was standing in his living room.

He put the sack of treasure on the table. Looking up at the ceiling he said

"It worked, it really worked."

"I knew you had doubts, Michael." He opened the sack and took out some of the treasure.

He picked up the gold statue of Tut that was taken from the small gilded shrine, the one that Howard Carter found empty. "This is the main thing I went back for." He fingered the statue and felt its weight.

"This thing could fetch a king's ransom on the open market." "But there's more money to be made my way." He took out all the other trinkets he took; there were several necklaces and lapis lazuli pins and gold, lots of gold. There was also a cosmetic box and writing instruments.

"Tomorrow we take these to the Metropolitan Museum of art and get the ball rolling."

Mike put the statue down and walked into the bedroom, he changed out of the ninja outfit, put it away in the closet with the rest of the gear. While he was changing he looked up at the ceiling and said.

"Boy, that air horn really scared the shit out of them didn't it?"

"Yes Michael, it did."

"Hell I bet it could have been heard on the other side of the river."

"It was, the people in the village said that the gods had discovered the thieves and thought that they would be coming to the village to punish their families also." "When the men returned to the village and told everyone what had happened, it was another three years before anyone went into the valley to rob a tomb."

"How do you know all that?"

"I stayed there after I sent you here to watch what happened."

Mike walked out of the bedroom and headed for the kitchen, opened fridge and took out a beer.

"I haven't made any plans past wanting to take these to the museum, I mean like who to take them to."

"I guess I could just walk into the place and ask for someone in charge of the Egyptian wing."

Mike was sitting at the dining room table and looking up at the ceiling.

"My friend, we have to do something about my always looking up at the ceiling."

"I mean if I'm out some place and I want to talk to you, people are going to think I'm crazy when I look up to the sky and start talking, know what I mean?"

"Yes Michael, I know what you mean."

"I can produce for you what on your world would be called a holographic figure."

"I know what a hologram is, but what is a holographic figure?"

"This is a holographic figure Michael." And standing before Mike in the living room was a man. Dressed in a hunting outfit, rifle and all.

"What the- who are you?" the figure looked at Mike and smiled but didn't say anything.

"That is the holographic figure I was telling you about."

Mike got up from the table and walked over to the man standing in the living room. He reached out to touch the figure but his hand went right through the man.

"I can make the figure have substance, I can make it solid so you can feel it and it will look real to all who see it."

"Does is have to be a man?"

"No Michael, it can be anyone or anything you want it to be."

Mike was walking around the figure and giving it the once over, he asked.

"Let me see a female figure."

And there before him in the place of the man was standing a female, also dressed as a hunter.

"I'm partial to blondes, can you make about four or five that I can choose from?"

"Yes." Before he could blink, there were five blondes standing before him, all hunters.

"Look, can we forget the hunting outfits?"

And in the blink of an eye all the figures were naked.

Mike jumped back.

"Whoa." He slowly walked around the five figures before him. He was thinking out loud to himself when he said.

"Now this is something I can get used to."

Now the alien voice in his head spoke to him and said

"If you want to have sex with any or all of them, just touch the one you want and she will become real."

Mike looked up at the ceiling and smiled.

"You're kidding, right?"

"No Michael, I am not kidding."

Mike reached out and touched one blonde on the shoulder. She had substance, she was real. She reached over to Mike and put her arms around him. Mike let himself be led into the bedroom. About 30 minutes later. The two of them were standing in the living room again; Mike looked up at the ceiling and said.

"Okay my friend, I've chosen the companion I want."

"Good Michael, now what would you like to do?" He looked at the figure he just got out of bed with.

"Did you just speak to me?"

"Yes Michael, I am now speaking through this figure, you will no longer look up to speak to me, I will respond through this girl."

"You mean you're no longer up there?" He said pointing up to the ceiling.

"No Michael I'm still up here only I will be speaking through this figure."

"Okay, that sounds good to me, but right now I need some sleep, tomorrow we can go to the museum and get things started."

"Can you get me up around eight o'clock?"

"Yes Michael." Mike started to walk back to the bedroom.

"You stay here and guard the treasure, I assume you don't need sleep?"

"I will stay here and guard the treasure Michael." Mike stopped and turned around

"One more thing before I turn in, I have to give you a name."

"I never knew a girl named Susan, so I think I'll call you Sue."

Mike felt someone pushing him.

"Wake up Michael, it's eight o'clock."

"What, oh yeah, it's you."

"I was kind of thinking this was all a dream." Mike was expecting to hear the voice in his head and he looked up to the ceiling again.

"No Michael, I'm here now, remember?"

"Yeah, yeah I remember, where's the treasure?"

"It's still here."

"Good, look, I'm going to take a shower and make something to eat, then we can get started."

"Whatever you want to do Michael."

"Look, Sue, while I'm in the shower, could you look up in the phone book and see if you can find out who's in charge at the museum?"

"Sure Michael, anything you want." Mike looked at the girl, she was still naked.

"It seems we forgot to get you dressed last night, I hope you're not cold?"

"No Michael, I'm not cold."

"Well how come you didn't get dressed?"

"You didn't tell me to."

"I didn't think I had to, look, whip yourself up something to wear, I'll be right out." With that Mike walked into the bathroom.

"Well I have to give you credit, you sure did dress up nice." He stood there looking at Sue,

"I like the outfit, yeah, you did a great job."

"I looked through your memory and picked out something I thought you would like."

"Well you did a great job." Sue had dressed herself in a short pleated skirt, red and a white short sleeve blouse, no stockings and a pair of penny loafers.

"Did you find out anything about the museum?"

"Yes Michael, I have the phone number of a Mr. James O'Brien, he's in charge of the Egyptian wing at the Met."

"Good, let me get dressed and then we'll call and tell him we're coming over with something he'll be interested in." Mike walked into the bedroom and started to get dressed. He looked around and Sue was standing there.

"Look Sue I know we were intimate last night, but you can't follow me around like this."

"Why not."

"Because a girl doesn't stand around and watch while a man gets dressed."

"Your planet and culture are very strange Michael, I have dealt with thousands of planets in your galaxy, and yours is by far the most backwards."

"What do you mean by that?"

"Never have I seen a culture so caught up in sex and yet so ashamed to be naked in front of the opposite sex."

"Okay, ok hang around if you want, I really don't care."

Mike reached over and picked up the phone from the nightstand next to his bed and handed it to Sue.

"Here make the call and ask to speak to Mr. O'Brien."

The phone started to ring, Mike walked over and took the phone from Sue.

"Good morning, Dr. O'Brien's office."

"Good morning, I hope I have the right office, I have some Egyptian antiquities I'd like to give to the museum."

"Could you hold on for a minute please?"

"Yes of course." Mike put his hand over the receiver and spoke to Sue.

"I think we got the right office." Miss Parker pushed the hold button and spoke to Dr. James O'Brien, head of the Egyptian section of the Metropolitan museum.

"Dr. I have someone on the phone that wants to give some Egyptian antiquities to the museum."

"Tell him to call back on Monday an make an appointment, I've got to catch a plane."

Miss Parker pushed the button and spoke to Mike.

"I'm sorry, Dr O'Brien can't see you today, but if you would call back on Monday and make an appointment, he would be glad to see you next week." Mike looked at Sue and then back at the phone.

"ER, that's ok, I'll be right over." And he hung up the phone.

"Can you get us over to the museum before that guy leaves?" And before Mike could blink, they were standing outside of Dr. O'Brien's office.

"I wish you wouldn't do that."

"Sorry Michael, but you wanted to get here fast." Mike knocked on the door with Dr. O'Brien's name on it. Miss Parker walked over and opened the door.

"Yes, can I help you?"

"Hi, my name is Michael and I just spoke to you on the phone about some antiquities."

"And I really didn't want to wait until next week."

"How did you get over here so, I mean I just hung up the phone." Miss Parker was thoroughly confused and was holding onto the doorknob as Mike and Sue walked past her, Mike walked over to the desk and put the box of treasure down.

"Can I assume your O'Brien?" Mike asked putting his hand out.

"Yes I'm Dr. O'Brien, but I really don't have time right now I'm on my way to the airport, I have to catch a plane."

"I'll be returning on Wednesday and I'll be more than happy to see you then."

"Well Doc, I think you'll postpone your little trip when you see what I have here." And with that said Mike opened the box and removed the gold statue of Tutankhamen and placed it on the desk.

James O'Brien's field of expertise was ancient Egypt; he was about to protest a little more firmly at this intrusion. But when he saw the statue that Mike pulled out of the box, his eyes widened a little. He reached over and picked it up from the desk. Mike continued to empty the box and place the treasures on desk. Dr. O'Brien was looking from the statue in his hand to the treasure on the desk.

"Where did you get this."

"I took these from the thieves that were stealing them from the tomb of king Tut." Dr. O'Brien was paying more attention to the statue in his hands and the treasure on the desk than to what Mike was saying. Miss Parker was now over at the desk and was picking up different pieces and looking at them. She had been working at the museum under Dr. O'Brien for four years now and had picked up some knowledge about antiquities.

"I'm sorry, where did you say you got these from?"

"I took them from the thieves that were taking them from Tut's tomb." Dr. O'Brien looked at Mike.

"Tuts tomb was opened in 1925, you can't be older than 45."

"Everyone associated with the opening of the sealed door is dead now."

"I assure you Doc, I took all this stuff from three men in Tuts tomb, they had made hole in the upper left corner of the sealed door and one of them had squeezed through, I came upon them before they could escape with all this." Mike said gesturing with his hand at the treasure on the desk. Dr. O'Brien was convinced what he had in his hands was the missing statue from the gilded shrine in Tuts tomb, but he was not quite convinced at Mikes explanation."

"The valley of the kings and especially Tuts tomb are guarded night and day by the Egyptian Government, there is no way for anyone to break into the tomb, and besides the only treasure left in the tomb is the outer most coffin an tuts body."

"Are you saying there was another room the Carter didn't see and someone else just found it?"

"No, I'm saying I interrupted a robbery and took this stuff before it disappeared from history."

Dr. O'Brien was confused, but still interested in these objects from Tuts tomb. He asked Mike again.

"Let me get this straight, you took this stuff from some thieves and then took it out of Egypt, through customs without being caught?"

"Before I answer that question, tell me, is the museum interested in all this, or do I take it to Boston?" Dr. O'Brien looked at the treasure, which he knew was real and back to Mike.

"If this is real and the price is right, we might be interested."

"Doc, let's not beat around the bush, you know the stuff is real."

"And like I said, it's not for sale, I want to give it to the museum." Dr. O'Brien and Miss Parker looked at each other, each holding some of the treasure and trying to figure this whole thing out.

"Miss Parker would you please call Boston and tell them I won't be coming today, then call the airport and cancel my reservation." Miss Parker put down the necklace she was holding and picked up the phone.

"Yes Dr. O'Brien."

"I didn't catch your name?" Dr. O'Brien said holding out his hand for Mike to shake it.

"Oh, I'm sorry Doc, My name is Mike, no last names yet, and this is my assistant Sue."

"Very pleased to meet you Mike, and Sue." Dr. O'Brien gave Sue the once over from head to foot. He put his hand out for Sue to shake.

"Very pleased indeed."

"And I'm pleased to meet you Dr. O'Brien, would you like to have sex with me?"

All eyes in the room turned to Sue.

"Sue." Mike grabbed her and took her aside.

"What are you saying, you can't just say things like that." Sue looked at Mike

"But I read it in his eyes when he looked at me."

"I don't care, You don't say things like that, I'll explain later." Mike turned back to Dr. O'Brien.

"I'm sorry Doc, Sue isn't from around here and she's not quite used to our customs yet."

Dr. O'Brien looked at Sue and then at Mike.

"Er, that's alright, no harm done." Miss Parker hung up the phone and looked at her boss a little confused.

"Dr., Boston said it would be alright and to call when you can come up."

"Mike, how did you get these past Egyptian customs without being caught?"

"Doc, I have never been to Egypt, and I didn't go through any bodies customs."

"Now you're really confusing me, you got these from the tomb, yet you've never been in Egypt." Dr. O'Brien looked at his secretary and then back to Mike.

"Would you like to make that a little clearer?"

"I mean if we accept these and then put them on display, the Egyptian government is going to come down on us real hard." Dr. O'Brien picked up a necklace and was examining it closely.

"I can tell you that they will make it very hard for all of our people we have now in Egypt."

"They can cancel dig permits and refuse us new ones and accuse our people of smuggling."

James O'Brien looked at Mike and Sue, he was very serious. He knew the treasure before him was real. But at the same time he was very aware of the consequences of displaying smuggled antiquities, especially any from the tomb of king Tut.

"Okay doc, let me explain a little further." Mike moved some papers aside and sat on Miss Parker's desk.

"I said I've never been in Egypt, and I haven't"

"But I have been in Kemit." Mike stopped and looked at Dr. O'Brien to see what kind of reaction that would get.

"You're playing with words Mike, Kemit was the name of ancient Egypt, but they are still the same place."

"No not exactly Jimmy."

"Can I call you Jimmy?" Dr. O'Brien was getting a little annoyed and it started to show.

"Look, Mike, if you're playing with me, you can take your trinkets and leave. I've got a plane to catch."

"Take it easy Jimmy, let me ask you this, do you believe in time travel?"

"Time travel?" Now Dr. O'Brien was getting pissed off, he almost believed this clown; he even canceled a plane to Boston. He put the necklace down and said.

"Look, I've got to get to Boston today and you've delayed me long enough."

"Miss Parker please call the airport and try to get me on another flight." Mike put his hand on Dr. O'Brien's arm and said

"I can see you're going to need a little proof."

Mike turned to Sue.

"Sue could you put us somewhere near the great pyramid of Kufu, not to close but not too far away either, you know what I want."

"Yes Michael." And with that said, all four people in the room were transported in less than the blink of an eye to the site of the pyramid of Kufu.

"Eeeeek," Miss Parker gave out a scream.

"What happened, where are we?" Miss Parker ran over to Dr. O'Brien who was staring open mouthed at the pyramid.

"Well what do you think Jim, is it real?" Dr. O'Brien looked around then turned to Mike.

"How do you, I mean is this real?"

"Of course it's real Jim, look around don't you feel the heat?"

"Look over there Jim, I bet you didn't think that was the way they built that? Mike was pointing to the pyramid in the distance. He reached down and picked up two handfuls of sand and dropped them on the desk.

"Here, feel the sand, smell the odor of ancient Egypt, drink in the sites of the past."

"Some ones coming, look." Miss Parker was point at three guards that had noticed the four of them standing where no one was supposed to be. The guards started to run towards them, they were shouting and getting closer. All turned to see the three Egyptian guards and Mike said.

"Okay Sue, get us out of here." As Mike spoke the guards were close enough for one of them to throw his spear. As the four travelers returned to the museum, the spear followed them and embedded itself in the wall behind Dr. O'Brien's desk. The noise made both Jim and Miss Parker turn around and look.

"What the hell was that all about."

"I mean, how the hell did you do that, I mean was it real." Dr. O'Brien was clearly confused; he was asking the questions and looking around not sure if he had seen what he had seen.

"That was an illusion, wasn't it, who the hell are you any way."

Mike walked over to the spear in the wall and yanked it out.

"You know our names Dr. O'Brien, all the rest will come in time."

"Now let me ask you again, are you interested in this treasure or do I take it to the Boston museum?"

Mike placed the spear on the desk in front of Jim. Miss Parker asked.

"What happened Jim, what happened and where did those men come from?"

Jim O'Brien, looked at his secretary and at the sand and the spear on his desk, he ran his fingers through the sand and picked up the spear.

"The sand and the spear are still warm, I don't know how you did it, but I'm convinced you did it."

"Did what?" Miss Parker was still confused. Mike got closer to Jim and asked.

"Are you convinced you traveled through time?"

"I'm not sure, but I guess we did." O'Brien sat down in his chair and ran the sand through his fingers.

Miss Parker excused herself, saying she had to go to the lady's room. Jim still thoroughly confused sat there with his brow wrinkled deep in thought.

"Why did you come to me, to this museum?"

"When I was a teenager, I would spend many happy hours walking through the Egyptian wing, it's one of my favorite places." Dr. O'Brien was alternating his attention between the treasure and the spear and sand. He was deep in thought.

"You know Mike, I'm finding it hard to understand that this is the missing treasure from Tut's tomb."

"That I'm holding in my hands the statue that Howard Carter found missing from the gilded shrine?"

Mike picked up one of the necklaces and said.

"Yeah, I know what you mean, I get a kind of thrill from holding this in my hands knowing that Tut wore this around his neck." Jim put the statue down and looked up at Mike.

"So, what are you asking for this priceless treasure."

"How many times must I tell you I'm not selling it, I donating it to the museum."

"Okay, let's say we except the treasure, and put it on display."

"Can you imagine how much heat we will get from the Egyptian government?" Mike looked at Jim and then at Sue.

"Why would they say anything at all?"

"Think Mike, we would be accused of smuggling stolen treasure out of Egypt."

"They would cancel our dig permits, harass our people in the field, accuse them of stealing from them."

"And generally make life miserable for all our people in Egypt." Mike changed the subject.

"Let me think on that."

"Suppose someone offered you the opportunity to travel back in time and sit in the Roman coliseum and watch the gladiators fight, or sit on a hill and watch, from a safe distance, the siege of Troy."

"Or maybe you wanted to take a camcorder back and tape the British surrender at York Town."

"I would charge a fee for that, think of the money that could be made." Jim thought for a moment.

"But how would you find somebody that would be interested enough and rich enough to make you any money?"

"I'm not greedy Jim, I just want enough to live comfortable on and know where I can get more when I need it, know what I mean."

"Yeah, I get the idea, but the question still stands." Mike stood up and picked up the spear from the desk. He walked over to the entrance to Jim's office.

"Did you ever wonder how much treasure Ramses was buried with, or what Akhenaten tomb looked like before it was destroyed?"

"Just how much would it be worth to you to go back and find out?"

Jim looked at the treasure before him and said.

"If I could afford it Mike, I'd jump at the chance, but how much are you considering asking for such a trip?"

"And if the price was right I know I could come up with the names of at least a dozen others who would give up their first born to take such a trip."

"Well to be perfectly honest with you, I haven't thought about it yet." Mike turned to his female companion and asked.

"Sue I'm sure you've gone through this before, how much should I charge?"

"Michael, I have been doing this since long before you're galaxy was formed."

"The beings I have dealt with have varied in intelligence and development between the earliest civilizations on your planet and where mankind will be a million years from now."

Sue continued

"Some have used my power to help their worlds; others have used it to bring down empires."

"Charges have ranged from free service to demands for vast fortunes, control of worlds to slavery of individuals or whole worlds." Mike interrupted.

"And you've gone along with this slavery of worlds?"

"Yes Michael, I do not have free will like you, I do as I am told to do."

"Remember I told you those who sent me out gave me a mission, and it's purely entertainment to them." Mike shook his head and turned back to Jim.

"Well Jim, I guess I'll have to come up with a price on my own, Sue's no help at all."

Jim was looking through the treasure before him; he looked up at Mike and said.

"You know Mike, the more I think about this time travel, the more excited I get."

"The knowledge that could be gained would be priceless."

Mike felt the line jerk and knew he had his first bite.

"I think I felt a bite on my line Jim, are you interested?"

"You know I am, that glimpse you gave us before of Kufu's pyramid was enough to wet my appetite."

"But Mike, before I commit myself, I have a friend who works here, Irving Sussman, we're both into ancient Egypt, I know he'd be interested in a trip, but I'd like to speak to him first."

"Okay Jim, when do you expect him?"

"He should be here any time now, why don't you and Sue take a walk around the museum for awhile, when he comes I'll send someone to come and get you."

"Better yet, here." Mike handed Jim his card with his beeper number on it.

"When he arrives, call us, we'll be in the Egyptian wing."

"Okay Mike, and while you're gone, think of a price, but remember, we're not rich."

Mike smiled and turned to leave with Sue.

"Wait Mike, here use these passes to get in, I don't want you should have to pay."

"Thanks Jim, we'll be waiting for your call."

Miss Parker returned from the lady's room and pulled up a chair next to Dr. O'Brien's desk. Mike turned to Sue.

"What do you think Sue, Jim makes some valid points here."

"Michael you are free to make any decision you want concerning this venture of yours."

"Yeah, I know, but I'm only asking for a little input from you." Jim and Miss Parker were fingering the various pieces of jewelry and turned their attention to Mike and Sue.

"The universal power that created you gave you free will to do as you please."

"You are responsible for your actions and eventually must answer for them."

I'm here to do as you say, not to decide for you." The answer took Mike by surprise.

Jim was trying to sort through what he had just heard; he looked from Sue to Mike and said.

"Universal power, what is she talking about Mike?"

"It's a long story Jim, just because Einstein said time travel was possible, doesn't mean someone from Earth was the first to develop it." Now Miss Parker and Jim looked at each other again and at Sue.

"You mean to tell me that she's an alien?" Jim asked pointing at Sue.

"In so many words, yes." Jim sat there looking from the treasure and the spear and sand on his desk and at Sue, his mind was racing, trying to sort through it all.

Mike took advantage of the lull in questioning to try and figure out his next move.

Should he give the treasure to the museum anyway and risk an international incident. And in doing so, put the museums people in the field at risk. Or should he go ahead and sell it on the black market, this stuff would bring a small fortune. Jim broke the silence.

"I would hate to let this slip through the museums fingers, but there is no way to display it without getting flak from Egypt." Mike was thinking and after a couple of minutes of silence.

"You know there just may be a way." Jim looked up at Mike.

"I'm all ears Mike."

"Well, suppose it was willed to the museum by an unidentified person."

"Go on Mike, but who?"

"Someone that was at the opening of the tomb with Carter, someone who had sticky fingers."

"Yeah, but the last person that was at the opening died years ago." Mike thought for a minute.

"Okay, so in their will, they stipulated that the release of the treasure to the museum take place Twenty years after their death?" Jim was thinking and still holding onto the statue from the shrine like it belonged to him. He smiled like a light bulb came on in his head.

"Yeah, twenty years and the law firm releases it and no names are given to protect their clients anonymity."

"I like the way you think Mike, you got a deal." Miss Parker spoke.

"Jim I think to make everything legal, someone would have to make up some papers to make the transfer of the treasure to the museum at least look legal."

Mr. O'Brien looked at his secretary and said

"Okay, that makes sense, what do you think Mike, know anybody that can do that?"

Mike turned to Sue and asked.

"Sue, can you do that, make up some legal papers that would fool the Egyptian Gov't. if they got nosey?" And before anyone moved, Sue pointed to Jim's desk. Jim looked at the papers that just appeared on at the corner of the desk.

"I'll be-how the hell does she do that Mike." He was thumbing through the papers and commented.

"I'll be damned, this is amazing, their real, I mean their authentic."

"How did you do that so fast Sue?" Mike answered

"She has a knack for doing things fast." Jim stood up and put his hand out to Mike.

"On behalf of the museum, I want to thank you and Sue, but what are you getting out of this Mike?"

"Well Jim, I had something else in mind besides these few trinkets."

"Like what Mike?" Jim asked a little apprehensively. "I'll let you know when I figure something out."

As Mike and Sue left Dr. O'Brien's office, Janet, Miss Parker turned to her boss and said.

"Well what the hell do you make of that?"

"I have to admit it's the strangest start to a day I've ever had." They were going through the jewelry and treasure left behind by Mike and Sue. Janet turned to Jim and asked.

"Do you think Irving will buy what happened here today?"

"I've been thinking about that. The story is a little hard to swallow, but you can't argue with this."

Jim held up the golden statue of King Tutankhamen that had been taken from the tomb in antiquity.

"This is the real thing, I'd bet my life on it, Irving will agree, I know him."

Just then the phone rang. Miss Parker picked up the receiver.

"Hello, Mr. O'Brien's office can I help you?"

"Hello, Janet, this is Irving, I can't make it today, there's just too much traffic out here and the car is acting up. Is Jim there?" Janet handed the phone to Jim.

"Hi, Irv, can't make it today heh?"

"Sorry Jim, just too much traffic and like I told Janet, my cars acting up, so I'm just going to turn around and go home, see you tomorrow."

"Irv, something very strange and very exciting has happened, you've got to come in tomorrow, it's extremely important,"

Don't worry, I'll be there, but what happened?"

"I can't tell you over the phone, just get here as early as you can, Janet and I will be very busy today and will probably stay the night in the guest room."

"Wow, this must be important, Okay, I'll be there early, see you then." And Irving Hung up.

Dr. O'Brien paged Mike, and asked him if he would come back tomorrow, that something had come up and nothing could be done until Mr. Sussman arrived in the morning. Mike agreed.

Saturday morning Irving Sussman arrived at the museum at 0630, the guards let him in and he went to the spare room that was set up as a small apartment for occasions when any member of the staff had to stay in town. Or when something big was happening at the museum. Janet and Jim went to bed late. They spent most of the night going over the treasure and trying sort it out and catalog it. After they ate a late supper, they retired.

Irving Sussman knocked on the door to the apartment.

"Come on in Irv." He heard Jim answer. Janet opened the door and let him in. Irving looked around.

"Okay, what's so damned important that I had to get up at four o'clock to get here?"

"Yeah, good morning to you to." Jim said

"Let's go to my office, everything is over there." Jim motioned to Irving and Janet to follow him. They left the apartment and walked down the hall to the privet elevator that took them down to the office complex in the basement of the museum. When they had entered Jim's office, Jim and Janet walked over the desk were the treasure was covered by a plane white sheet.

"This is what I told you about, that's so damned Important." And with that Jim pulled the sheet off and exposed the treasure. Irving Sussman walked over the desk and stood there looking at all the gold. His mouth opened slightly. He picked up the statue of Tutankhmen and turned it around in his hands.

"Where did you get this from?" He, like Jim and Janet before him at first seeing everything, his eyes kept moving from one piece to another, he didn't know what to pick up first.

"Wait a minute, this stuff can't be real, it's practically new." He held a necklace out to Jim.

"Oh its real alright, I can vouch for its authenticity." Jim stood there smiling.

"Look, Jim, I know artifacts when I see them, and these look like they were made last week."

"In a way you're not far from right Irv." Jim picked up the statue that Irving had put down.

"Here, look at this statue, right here." Jim said pointing to the very bottom of the statue.

"You can see the red tint in the gold, right here around the heel. They still haven't gotten all the impurities out of the gold." "If that had been made recently, you wouldn't have that, and besides, this thing is solid gold, solid gold Irv." Irving looked at the point where Jim had been pointing.

"Okay, the statue might be real, but the jewelry, I know that's not 3500 years old."

"Your wrong Irv, its every bit 3500 years old, sit down and let me tell you what happened here yesterday." Jim and Janet related to Irving

Sussman all that had happened the day before down to the strange pair disappearing in front of them.

Back at Mike's house, Mike was sitting in his favorite chair trying to figure what to do to kill the rest of the day. He knew he could ask this alien to take him to the next day just to speed things up. But he figured he'd only be wishing his life away. So turning the TV on, Mike was surfing the channels, it was still early in the morning, nothing on but stupid talk shows. He turned off the boob tube and sat back. Sue walked over and sat on the arm of the chair.

"What would you like to do to kill the rest of the day Michael?"

"You're picking up the language very well Sue."

"Thank you Michael."

"And the way you act, you know lounging around sitting on the arm of the chair and being all friendly."

"If I didn't know you were an alien hologram, I'd swear you were real."

"That is part of my programming Michael, to blend into and become part of the life of the planet that I'm on."

"Well you do it very well, you're a credit to your makers."

"Are they still watching what's going on?"

"No Michael, the galaxy I came from has long since disappeared."

"So how come you're still out here doing this?"

"They never called me back, and since I'm indestructible and my power is eternal, I'll go on forever."

"You mean you'll be doing this until the end of time?"

"Time as you call it Michael, will never end, but yes I'll go on forever."

"Gee, that's sad Sue, I don't know what to say."

"Don't feel sorry for me Michael, I have no feelings or emotions, I'm only a machine."

Mike looked up at Sue and smiled, he thought to himself, "You're real to me Sue and my heart is saddened by what you've told me anyway."

Sue knew his thoughts, but chose not to respond, the human race was certainly a strange one.

Deep in thought, Mike sat there just staring at the blank screen. There were so many things he had always wanted to do. He jumped when the light bulb came on in his head

"Oh yeah, now I remember what I always wanted to do."

Sue looked down at him and said

"You want to return to you sophomore year in high school and get even with the class bully."

"How did you––Oh yeah I keep forgetting you're reading my thoughts."

"But you're right, can you make it happen Sue?"

"Yes Michael, you must remember there is nothing I can't do."

"You sound like you were given the power of the gods Sue." Sue looked at him and smiled Mike didn't know what to make of her reply; he just looked at her and said.

"Yeah, right."

"Any way, how do we, um, you do it?" Sue stood up and walked over to the armchair and sat down.

"Michael, you want to return to you younger body and spend a couple of days back in high school just to take revenge on the class bully, is that right?"

"That's it in a nut shell."

"Okay, when do you want to go and where would you like to start?"

"You can put me in my old body without any trouble?"

"I will put you into your younger self and there will be no discomfort on your part, neither of you will suffer any harm." "In fact when you return, you're younger self will have gained all your knowledge up to today."

"You mean my younger self will be better off because of my return?"

"Yes Michael, you will have given your younger self knowledge, strength, and self confidence."

"All in all a great gift." Mike thought for a second and then said.

"Well what are we waiting for, let's go."

"I will not return with you Michael, I will remain here with your body."

"Wait a minute, my body?"

"Yes Michael, I will send back your soul only."

"My soul, you can do that?"

"Yes."

"Yeah yeah I know, you can do anything."

The return was so sudden it took Mike by surprise as usual. He tripped up the stairs from the suddenness of it and heard a laugh from behind. Mike turned around and looked into the face of his nemesis. He was trembling with anticipation, but didn't do anything he just turned back and continued to his class.

As he walked down the hall he was trying to contain his excitement, here he was back in 1956, he was trying to drink in all the sights as fast as he could and in doing so walked right passed the classroom. He realized he had already started to "down load" information with his younger self, and this sharing of information made him stop and enter the English class. Mike walked into the class and saw several of the other students already seated and the teacher, Miss O'Connell standing at the desk greeting the students as they entered.

"Good morning Michael." Mike was taken by surprise; his teacher was prettier then he remembered or was it the fact that he was looking at her through more mature eyes.

"Good morning Miss O'Connell." Mike answered and continued on to his seat. The next to the last seat in the isle by the window. He put his books under the seat and took out the English book laid it on the desk and took out his blue pen and put on the desk as well. Mike looked up and saw the bully, Robert Crowley, come in and sit behind him. It didn't take the bully long to start in; he took out a pencil and jabbed Mike in the shoulder.

"Good Morning Miss O'Connell." He mimicked Mike

"You like her don't you pussy boy?" Mike was biding his time.

"I heard you say you'd like to see her tits."

"Now if you give me your pens, I'll forget what I heard, otherwise I'm going to tell her."

Robert Crowley put out his hand expecting Mike to hand over the pen. The teacher started roll call before starting the class. Mike hadn't reacted to the demands for the pen and Robert was getting annoyed.

He picked up his pencil and again jammed it into Mike's back, just then the teacher called.

"Michael Griener?"

"Here" Mike answered raising his hand. And then he did the unexpected.

"Excuse me Miss O'Connell."

"Michael, please let me finish the roll call."

"Miss O'Connell, this is very important." Robert started to get nervous. He whispered into Mike's ear from behind."

"If you say anything pussy boy, I'll get you after school."

"What is it Michael?"

"Please excuse me for interrupting the class, so I'll make this as brief as possible."

"Yes Michael what is it." The teacher was getting annoyed at this unusual interruption.

Mike turned around and with speed his younger self didn't know he possessed, he grabbed Robert by the neck and picked him up from the seat. An audible gasp escaped from the class and Miss O'Connell yelled, but he didn't hear anything but his own voice. Mike turned red as he spoke to Robert.

"Look punk, I've taken all I'm going to take from you, now I'm going to meet you after school across from the main entrance and bring your friends, because you're going to need them." By this time the teacher was there.

"Michael let go of him, what's come over you?" Mike released his grip on Bob's neck and he dropping him into his seat.

"I beg your pardon Miss O'Connell." Then he turned to the class and said

"I'm sorry for the interruption, then again turning to the teacher he pointed to his back. There was a red stain on his shirt getting bigger from the blood oozing out of his shoulder. The teacher gasped.

"Michael, how did this happen?" Mike pointed his finger at the bully and said.

"He jabbed me with his pencil, twice." Miss O'Connell turned to Robert Crowley and asked."

"Did you do that?" Bob Crowley taken completely by surprise at the strength of this kid he had been bulling for weeks, just sat there rubbing his sore neck.

"Go ahead, be the man your pretending to be and admit it." Mike said looking Bob right in the eye.

The bully, looking first at Mike and then at the teacher, shook his head no.

The teacher knew he was lying, and said.

"That's it, the both of you to the dean's office."

"Michael, you better go to the nurses office and get that taken care of." Mike smiled at the teacher and said.

"It's okay Miss O'Connell, I'll be alright, and if you will allow me, I promise you there will be no more interruptions from ether of us, ever again, you have my word on it."

Miss O'Connell really wanted to get the class going, she looked at them both and said.

"Okay, but this is the last time, I will not tolerate any disturbance, the next time you both go to the dean's office, do you understand?"

"Yes ma'am" Mike said and they both looked at Bob Crowley still rubbing his neck. He looked at the teacher and shook his head yes. The teacher turned and walked to the front of the classroom. Mike looked at the stunned bully and said.

"3:10 out front, don't forget." And he sat down. When the class ended, Mike got up and walked out into the hall. He turned left and headed for the gym, his next class. He was trying to look at everything and everyone at the same time. Seeing friends he had forgotten and just being happy at returning to his old school. Mike walked slowly down the hall and stopped at one of the bulletin boards to read what was going on. In the meantime, Robert Crowley stepped out of the class and stood waiting in the hall for one of his gang members to come along. Bob Crowley was a senior and 2 to 3 years older than Mike, he couldn't figure out how or what went wrong.

"I'm older and stronger than pussy boy."

"It had to be a fluke, he just caught me off guard." He was trying to justify what went wrong in the class, for the last couple of weeks, since the term started he'd been pushing this guy around. It had been fun, the kid was a real pussy, once he almost had him crying. So what went wrong?

Mark Roberts, the second in command of the gang walked up to Robert Crowley.

"Hey man what's new?"

"I'll tell you what's new." And Bob related to Mark what had taken place in the classroom.

"Fuck 3:o'clock, let's get him now." Mark said hitting his right hand fist into the palm of his left hand. He was looking around trying to see Mike.

"Do you know where he is now?" Mark asked.

"I think his next class is gym, he should be down that way somewhere."

They started to walk in the direction of the gym.

"There he is now." Bob pointed to Mike standing by the bulletin board. Mike had gotten caught up reading and had forgotten about everything else. Bob and Mark walked up the Mike and Bob grabbed him by the shoulder an spun him around.

"Hey pussy boy, what the fuck was that you pulled in class?" he shoved Mike back against the wall.

"You hurt my neck and now I'm going to hurt you." Mike focused on the situation, now the jujitsu Mike had been taken the last 3 years was going to come in handy.

"Don't do that again." Mike said. Now Mark joined in and started to push Mike.

"Yeah, what are you going to do pussy boy?" Mark asked. Now the bully was laughing and the other kids in the hall were watching.

When Bob pushed Mike again, Mike grabbed Bob's extended right hand and twisted it to Bobs left. Mike had more strength then expected so he had no choice but to bend to his left. Now bent over and at Mikes mercy, Bob couldn't do anything but wait, Mark, stunned by what he had just seen, stood there with his mouth open and Mike took the advantage and acted first. He kicked out with his right foot and caught Mark in the stomach and sent him across the hall into the wall. Mike looked at Bob and said.

"So you couldn't wait until after school could you punk, and being the brave punk you are you had to bring help."

"With a little more effort I could snap your arm at the shoulder, would you like that?" And for emphasis he twisted the arm some more. Wrenching with pain, Bob said.

"Stop, stop you're hurting me."

"Oh, am I?" "Let's see now, if you had me in this position, would you ease up?"

"I think not." And Mike twisted a little more. Bob started to cry with the pain. Mike eased up.

Mark leaning against the wall asked.

"Where did you learn that?"

"I read books." Just then Miss O'Connell came out of her room attracted by the commotion.

"Michael, Robert, you two again?"

"Let him go Michael." Holding onto his shoulder and holding back tears, Bob said.

"He attacked me again Miss O'Connell, I didn't do anything, honest."

"This time you going to the dean's office, both of you come along." Mark started to walk away. Mike said, grabbing Mark.

"Oh no you don't, you're in on this to."

"Who's this?" Miss O'Connell asked.

"These two attacked me." Mike said pointing to both Mark and Bob. He turned to all the students standing in the hall and asked.

"I don't suppose anybody saw what happened?"

"Would anyone care to tell the dean how I was attacked from behind by these two?"

All the students in the hall turned and started to walk away. Turning to the teacher, Mike said.

"I didn't think anyone would be brave enough to come forward."

Mike and the others started down the hall to the dean's office, Mr. Knowles. Mike knew the other kids in school were afraid of Bob and his gang, the Gents, that's what they called themselves. The Woodside gents. This was 1956 and there gangs all over the city. There must have been 5 or 6 different gangs in this school alone. But the biggest and baddest were the Woodside gents.

They were almost to the dean's office when a voice from behind said "I saw what happened Miss O'Connell." Everybody stopped and turned around. There stood one of the 10 oriental students in this 99% white middle class school. Johnny Chung was a junior; his parents moved from China town to Woodside 4 years ago. Johnny Chung was walking down the hall from the other direction when he saw Robert and Mark come up behind Mike. He saw them start the fight with Mike, and he wasn't going to say anything, but he saw Mike use the jujitsu on the bullies. He had to find out were Mike had learned it. It was unusual to find a white boy who knew the martial arts. Johnny's father was going to open a karate and jujitsu studio on Steinway Street in a month or so and he had to find out if there was another studio around that would give his father any competition.

Mike was surprised to find anyone brave enough to come forward.

"Then you come along also." Miss O'Connell said.

The way Bob and Mark looked at Johnny, if looks could kill he would have died right there.

Johnny paid no attention to their stares. He had a second-degree black belt in both Karate and Jujitsu; he could take care of himself.

The dean of boys, Mr. Knowles, was in his 40's. Balding and overweight. He had an untrimmed mustache and a deep voice that shook the very wall's when he raised it. He tried to dress neatly, but his large stomach was hard to hide. He was a strict disciplinarian and all the boys who crossed his path tried very hard to avoid a second crossing. Miss O'Connell opened the door to the dean's office and everyone filed in.

"What have we here Miss O'Connell?" Mr. Knowles asked.

The teacher related to the dean of boys everything that had happened in the last hour. She pointed to the dried blood on Mike's back as evidence to what she believed happened. Then she asked Johnny to tell Mr. Knowles what he had seen happen in the hall. Mr. Knowles took Johnny aside and asked him if he wanted to speak or was he afraid because Bob and Mark were in a gang. Johnny said he wasn't afraid and told the dean what he had seen. Mr. Knowles thanked Johnny and told him he could go to his next class, he gave him a late slip to cover his time. The dean sat back and thought for a minute. He knew Robert and his gang; their paths had crossed before. He had no doubt that Robert and Mark were the instigator in this case. He had suspended Bob before to no avail. These two and their gang were bad apples.

"Miss O'Connell, would you take Mike outside for a moment?" He wanted to talk to Bob and Mark first, then he would deal with Michael.

"Certainly Mr. Knowles." And she led Mike outside the dean's office. Dean Knowles looked at Bob and Mark he addressed Bob first.

"This is the third time you've been in my office this term, isn't it Bob?"

"Yes sir Mr. Knowles." Bob answered.

"The first time you were caught smoking in the bathroom."

"The second time you were fighting in the gym and now you're fighting in the hall."

"I've suspended you twice already this term, Mr. Crowley, if you can't keep your gang activities confined to the streets and alleys, you will find you're self permanently out of school."

The dean was looking at Bob, but the gang leader avoided his stare and looked at the wall.

"I don't think you really want that."

"When you put your mind to your school work, you get good grades."

"I wish I knew how to point you in the right direction."

Bob stood his hands crossed in front of him and Mark was following the direction of his leader.

"You're forcing me to give you another weeks suspension, the next time we meet under these circumstances, I'll start the process to put you out of school for good."

"Do you understand me Robert?"

"Yes sir Mr. Knowles." Now the dean turned his attention to Mark.

"And you Mr. Cross, this is your first visit to my office, am I right" Mark kept his eyes on the wall just like is leader.

"Yes Sir Mr. Knowles."

"You will receive the same punishment, do you understand Mr. Cross?"

"Yes Sir." The dean stood up and said.

"Mr. Cross, you would be well advised to choose your friends more carefully."

"You're suspensions start this coming Monday, now get out of here." As the two bullies left, Miss O'Connell entered with Mike. Mr. Knowles looked up at Mike.

"Michael Greiner, we've never met before have we?"

"No sir." Michael answered.

"From what I've seen and heard, you're the victim here."

"Anyone can be pushed to their limit, it happens all the time and I can't say I blame you for what you did."

"I hope you are aware of who you've made an enemy of today?"

"Yes Sir, I'm aware of the gang he leads, I'm not worried, I can take care of myself."

"I hope so Michael, keep your guard up, you can go."

"Thank you sir, I'll remember that."

Mike walked out of the dean's office and started to the gym, his next class. As Mike walked towards the gym he thought to himself. He was very happy the way things were working out. He knew his younger self would benefit from all his adult self knew. Like Sue had explained to him. Once he was inside his younger self, all the knowledge he had accumulated in life would be instantly down loaded" into his younger self. In a way he envied his younger self, because of all the information he would be picking up. As walked the hall way he thought.

"Sue, are you still here?"

"Yes Michael, I'm still here."

"Good, I was just checking." As Mike walked into the locker room he saw Johnny Chung changing into his sneakers and gym shorts. Johnny looked up to and saw Mike enter and Johnny smiled put out his hand.

"Hello again." Mike walked over to Johnny and shook his hand. Mike said

"I want to thank you for what you did back there, it took a lot of courage." Johnny smiled.

"It was nothing, what caught my eye was the jujitsu you were using."

"Do you have any belts?" Johnny asked.

"I only have a blue belt in jujitsu, but I have a brown belt in karate." Johnny was surprised.

"That's real good, where's your dojo?" Now Mike was stuck, what could he say. Thinking real fast, he said.

"I used to live in New Jersey, we just moved here awhile ago."

"I'm looking for a dojo around here, do you know of any?"

"My father is opening a Karate and Jujitsu studio on Steinway Street in a couple of weeks, why don't you come down and join us?"

"Okay, I'd like that." Johnny and Mike would be best friends from that day on.

Mike spent the rest of the school day enjoying the classes and telling his younger self all about his life. He told himself to work out and join the dojo, he mentioned all the mistakes he made in life, He instructed himself to avoid all of them. He said that the upcoming fight after school would have normally sent him home trembling, but to notice how calm he was and to watch how he handled it.

Three o'clock arrived and Mike was headed for the main entrance. Johnny offered to help, but Mike assured him everything would be ok. Johnny said he would be close just in case. Mike walked out the main door and sure enough there across the street was Bob and about five members of his gang.

Johnny looked at the assembled gang members and said

"There's to many of them let me help."

"No Johnny, this is my fight." Mike smiled and put his hand on his new friend's shoulder and walked across the street. Already a crowd had gathered, word travels fast. Mike put his books on a car and walked onto the sidewalk. He walked right up to Bob and said.

"Didn't get enough in school did you punk?"

"It's gonna be different this time pussy boy." Bob said as he stepped forward. Mike realized he was surrounded by all six of the gang members. And as he hoped, Bob through the first punch.

The speed of his older self and the agility of his younger self made a fine combination.

Mike blocked Bob's punch with a jujitsu hold that snapped Bobs elbow and sent him screaming to the ground. With spinning back kick, Mike caught Mark standing next to Bob in the stomach. The sight of their two leaders screaming and moaning on the ground from such a short and fast encounter sent the other four running. The other students couldn't believe what they had just seen. Most left, but some came up a patted Mike on the back. From his third floor window, Mr. Knowles smiled and picked up the phone and called an ambulance. Mike bent over Bob and said.

"I told you in English I wasn't gonna take any more of your bulling, but you had to push me and now you're paying for it."

"From now on when you see me walking down the street, you will be well advised to avoid me at all costs, do you understand me punk?" Bob holding his elbow and moaning with the pain replied.

"Yes, yes you broke my arm." Mike smiled and said

"And just what did you and your gang have in mind for me?"

"You got what you deserved." Mike stood up and walked over to Mark

Mark was still down on the ground, the kick caught him by surprise and it was so powerful he was throwing up. Mike looked him in the eye and said

"We've never met before today, why would you want to hurt me?"

"In the future, keep away from me, understand?" Mark looked at Mike and said

"Yeah, yeah I understand."

Mike went over to the car, picked up his books and started to walk home. Johnny came up and said.

"I'm very impressed Mike." Mike smiled at his new friend

"Thanks Johnny, coming from you, that's a real compliment."

"I can't wait to tell my father about this, I know he's gonna want to have you in the dojo."

"Yeah, I'm gonna like that Johnny, see you tomorrow."

Mike lived only a block from the school so the walk home was short. But today, Mike was taking his time. He was drinking in all he saw remembering the little things about the neighborhood he had forgotten. People and things he had not seen in forty years. There, there was the man who stood in the same spot every day at three o'clock and sold the salted pretzels, three for a quarter. And there across the street, the parking lot next to the old house that must have been there since the turn of the last century.

There was a little triangle park formed by the intersection of three streets, it had a bus stop and some benches so you could wait or just sit and relax. During the Second World War the park had a kind of bulletin board with the names of all the men in the area that were serving. And if one was killed, a gold star would be placed next to their names. As Mike approached the park he saw something that made him stop in his tracks. There sitting on a bench was the girl he would go out with for almost ten years. His heart started to beat a little faster, and he was sure his face had turned red. Now he remembered, she had told him, after they had been going out for a couple of years. That She and her mother would sit on the benches and wait for him to pass, she said that he always walked with his nose in the air.

Mike thought about it and couldn't remember ever seeing them sitting there. But now, faced with the problem of seeing them and knowing they know he sees them. He thought to himself. "God she's cute." And all kinds of memories came floating to the surface. They hadn't dated —yet, but they would. He wanted to stop and talk but couldn't work up the nerve. As he passed the bench, Mike smiled and kept waking. His heart was filled with love for her, a love he had thrown away.

Mike stayed for the night, he went over with his younger self all the mistakes he would make in the future, and all he had to do to avoid them. He hesitated when he heard his mother coming up the stairs to their second floor apartment, his mother had been dead for some twenty years now, and he didn't know if he could face her, at least his older self felt this way. Mike's faith in reincarnation helped him to decide to stay. He gave his mother the biggest kiss and hug he could work up.

"I love you mom, and I will always love you." His mother looked at him and said

"What was that all about, did you get the fish cakes from the deli like I told you?"

Mike slipped back to his own time and dimension sometime during the night.

He woke up in his own body, laid there for a time remembering people and friends who had already crossed over. And he started to cry, cry for his lost youth. Sue came in.

"Michael, you can return to your youth anytime you want." He wiped his eyes and looked at his genie.

"Yeah I guess you're right, I didn't realize how emotional a trip it would be."

"How much time passed Sue?"

"Five minutes Michael."

"That's all, five minutes?" Michael was stunned, he was there for almost a full day

"You could have stayed there a whole month and barley an hour would have passed."

"You didn't explain that, I spent about twelve hours there and only five minutes here?"

"How about me, did I age twelve hours?"

"No Michael, only five minutes." Mike sat on the edge of the bed and was thinking.

"Sue, suppose while I'm out of my body like just now, and something happens to the building I'm in, like an Earth quake, or fire or a war. What happens to my body?"

"Nothing will happen to your body Michael, I will protect it, I have powers you can't even imagine."

"Well that's good to know." Mike was sitting there thinking of all he has just experienced.

"Sue, I can't explain to you how happy I am, I just want to thank you for what you are doing for me."

You're welcome Michael."

Mike spent the rest of the day doing what he had originally planned to do before he met the alien; he went about without Sue, but kept in touch mentally. One other thing he did that was not on the agenda, he visited the grave of his mother.

After Jim had finished his story, Irving sat there looking at the two of them.

"I find it hard to believe that two intelligent people like you, could be caught up in a scam like this."

"What scam, there is no scam Irv. everything I've told you is the god's honest truth."

"You can't stand there and expect me to believe you went back in time?" Now Janet spoke.

"Yes Irving, we went back in time, there is no scam, they didn't ask us for a dime for this treasure."

Janet waved her hand over the mass of jewelry.

"No, they didn't ask you for any money for that stuff, but not yet they want a thousand dollars and hour to, as they say take you back in time to any place you want to go, that's the scam."

"Irving, look at the spear, that's genuine ancient Egyptian, fourth dynasty. You can't deny that."

"No, you're right, the spear and the statue look authentic, but I still have my doubts, I mean, time travel and aliens. Listen to what you're telling me Jim, it sounds so farfetched." Irv started to look through the jewelry again.

"Look Jim, you say their coming back Monday morning?"

"Yes, they're going to be here around eight or nine in the morning, I told Mike we would be ready then,"

"Okay Jim, I want to meet you're time travelers, let me talk to them before you hand over any money, Okay?"

"Okay Irv, just be here early Monday morning."

Monday morning at seven thirty, Irving Sussman was standing in Jim's office watching his friend and his secretary arranging things that they wanted to take back to the past with them. There were digital cameras, tape recorders, a camcorder. Irving walked over to the desk and was examining the treasure still lying around like so many paperweights.

"So, Jim, let me ask you something, if this is authentic like you say it is, why is it still on your desk instead on in the vault downstairs?" Jim O'Brien looked up from where he was dusting off a twelve gauge pump actions shotgun.

"To tell you the truth Irv, I just haven't gotten around to putting it away with all the excitement and getting ready for today."

"Yeah, well make me happy, and please put it some place were its going to be safe?"

"Okay, ok Irv, Janet will you put all that jewelry back in the box it came in, please?"

"Okay Jim, I'll get right on it." Irving Sussman was standing by the desk and looking at Jim when all of a sudden there were two people standing between them. Irv jumped and almost fell over.

"What the––who the hell?"

"Oh, hi Mike, Sue, I'd like you to meet my associate and friend Irving Sussman, Irving, this is the two people we were telling you about, this is Mike and this young lady is Sue, umm, the alien." Mike walked over to Irv and put out his hand.

"Hi Irv, pleased to meet ya." Irving Sussman stood there staring at but not believing what he saw.

"Hello Irving, Pleased to meet you too." Sue said extending her hand as Mike did.

"Yeah, yeah, pleased to meet you also." Irv said completely at a loss as to what he just saw.

"Where did you come from?" Irv asked Mike. Mike knew what Irving meant, but answered.

"I was born in NYC, but I'm living in New Jersey now, how about you?"

"No, no I mean, I mean you just popped in here, how did you do that? Did you use hypnotism on us?"

"No, no hypnotism, Sue here can do just about anything she wants." Mike knew he would have to spend some time explaining to Irv just what was going on.

"Jim didn't you tell Irving about us?"

"Yeah Mike, I told him everything, but we have a doubting Thomas with us." Mike turned to Irving and said.

"Well, I guess I'll have to prove to you what I proved to Jim and Janet here." And with that Mike turned to Sue and said.

"Sue take us to the Roman Coliseum, inside with the Christians." And in a heartbeat they were all standing among the Christians about to be devoured by the lions. There was screaming and crying and the roar of the hungry beasts about to gorge themselves on human flesh. No one noticed the new comers except for a couple of young children cowering under the parent's togas.

"My God." Janet said.

"Get us out of here, are you crazy?" She was clinging to Jim's arm. Jim and Irving were looking with horror at the scene before them. Irving was rubbing his eyes and trying to believe what he was seeing. All were visibly disturbed by what they were seeing. All of a sudden the lions charged, people were screaming and praying and trying to run away, but there was no place to run. Mike said

"Okay, Sue, let's get back." And again they were standing in Jim's office.

"Well Irv, what do you think?" Mike asked. Just as the lions charged, Irving pissed his pants. He looked down at the wet spot between his legs and trying to hide it looked up at Mike and said.

"How the fuck did you do that, I was never so scared and horrified in my life."

"So I noticed." Mike said pointing to the wet spot on Irv's pants, he turned to Sue and said.

"Sue, please clean that spot." Irving looked down and saw the spot disappear. Jim and Janet were still shaking with fright.

"Damn Mike, that was the scariest thing I've ever seen in my life, next time leave us here okay?"

"Sorry Jim, but I want to get the show on the road so to speak, and I thought that would be the quickest way to get done. Irv, if you're not convinced after that, I don't know how to prove it to you."

Irving Sussman was still shaking from the visual and emotional effect of what just happened.

"My God, that was the most horrible experience I've ever had, and it only lasted, what, five seconds?" Irving sat down in the chair by Jim's desk; he was almost on the brink of tears. Janet was in a state of shock, and Jim was leaning against the wall.

"I guess I picked the wrong place to take you back to." Jim looked at Mike and said

"I've read about those times and everybody knows that it happened, but to physically experience it is something else altogether. Those poor people, what a horrible way to have to die."

Janet was holding herself as if it was freezing and said.

"Did anyone see those two children that saw us? The ones peeking out from under their mothers toga?" Mike looked at Jim and Irving, both visibly scared and very effected by the brief trip, then he looked at Sue.

"I guess I picked the wrong time and place." Sue turned to others and said.

"The history of your planet is filled such scenes, people of one ethnic group or one city falling under the control or domination of another group or city and suffering torture and cruelty just because they were a little different, this is a very backward and violent planet. You shouldn't be so surprised at what you saw just now." Irving, Janet and Jim looked at Sue and back to each other.

"Your right Sue." Said Mike "We live in country that prides itself on being highly civilized and beyond such things as we just saw. Yet such horrors still exist in this world, maybe not so large a scale, but we all are aware of man's inhumanity to man." Irving looked at everyone and said.

"It makes you want to return to Rome and save those people, it would give me no greater pleasure than to put a shotgun up Nero's ass." That brought a little levity to the room. Jim had regained his composure and said.

"Well Irv, what do you think now?" Irving Sussman had also regained control of his emotions.

"What are we waiting for, let's go, I've always wanted to visit the temple of Luxor."

"Okay Mike, I've managed to scrape up three thousand dollars, that should be enough for a three hour trip back in time." Mike looked at Jim, and smiled.

"Yes, that will do nicely for three hours, but, where and when to you want to go?" Jim turned to his friend Irving and asked him.

"Well Irv, what do you think?" Irving Sussman was thinking for a second and said to Jim.

"Well Jim, to be honest, I could think of a hundred places I'd like to visit, but, it's your money, you decide, and because it's your money this time, next trip will be on me." Irv turned to Mike

"Is that Okay with you Mike, I mean if I can scrape up enough for another trip?"

"Sure Irv, anytime you want to go is all right with me."

Everyone burst into a flurry of activity, Jim and Janet started to check the back packs they had been fussing over when Mike and Sue dropped in. Irving started to check the cameras and with a renewed energy.

Jim was thinking as he rearranged the articles in his pack for the fourth time. He always wanted to find out exactly what did happen to king Tut. Every archeologist wanted to know just how was he killed, or did he fall and knock himself into a coma. He turned to Irving and asked

"Hey Irv, how about we return to Tut's final days and find out just how he did die?" Irv Sussman looked up from the camera and stopped what he was doing.

"Hey, I think you've got a good idea there Jim, yeah, that would be one hell of a trip."

Jim turned to Mike and Sue.

"Okay, Mike can you arrange it?" Mike looked at his alien genie. Sue shrugged her shoulders.

"Piece of cake, when would you like to go?" Mike shook his head in disbelief.

"You know Sue, you're turning into a real American, you're learning the vernacular very quickly."

"Thank you Michael." Mike turned to his three customers.

"Okay, you want to return to the day Tut bites the dust, is that right?"

"Yeah, but don't you think we should dress like them, I mean we'd kinda stand out like sore thumbs." Jim asked. Irving and Janet looked at themselves and how they were dressed and realized Jim was right.

"Yeah, your right Jim, I guess we should do a little more planning before we take the trip."

Mike looked at everyone and said.

"I've got a better idea, suppose we make this trip under a cloak of invisibility, we wouldn't have to change our clothes if no one could see us, would we?" Jim and Irving looked at each other and smiled. Both thought it was a good idea, and said so.

"Okay fellow travelers, are you ready?" Mike asked, Jim and Irving and Janet made minor arrangements of their clothing, as if they were getting ready to have their pictures taken.

"Okay Mike, we're ready." Jim thought for a moment and put his hand up to stop everything.

"Here Mike, I almost forgot." He pulled a white envelope out of his pocket; it contained three thousand dollars in twenties and fifties. Mike pointed to the desk behind Jim and said.

"Just leave it on the desk, Jim, I'll get it later." Jim turned and placed the money on his desk and turned back, looked at Mike and nodded.

Before the little group could blink, they were all standing in the chambers of the Pharaoh Tutankhamen. The suddenness of the move took them all by surprise. Sue arranged it so they would appear in the chamber in such a way as to be facing the people. No one spoke a word; it was like being in a theater when the curtain goes up, everyone stood still and quite.

There before them were Tutankhamen, his wife Ankhesenamen and four servant girls two of the girls were helping the king dress, one was standing by a table that had a pitcher of wine.

Another girl was standing by a table with a large bowl of fruit, waiting to serve the living god.

Ankhesenamen was pacing back and forth, she looked nervous. And every time she got near her husband, she would stop and speak to him in a tone that sounded like pleading.

Irv spoke first.

"Mike we can't understand them." Mike realized he had to ask Sue to let them understand the long dead language. Mike was about to ask Sue for a translation spell or whatever it was she did, when all six people in Tuts chamber stopped what they were doing and turned in the direction of the spoken word they had just heard. Irv spoke again.

"Uh oh, they can hear us." This time whispering. At that, the one girl by the fruit bowl ran screaming from the chamber. Which brought the two guards stationed outside Tuts chamber, running in with swords drawn and at the ready. Tut put up his hand to stop the guards and started to walk toward the spot where the voice came from. His wife stayed were she was and the three servant girls huddled together. Mike spoke, realizing something had to be done and done fast.

"Sue." Now all eyes shifted in his direction. The Pharaoh changed his direction and walked toward Mike. He bumped into Irving. Now he was told from the very first day he took the throne of the two lands that he was a living god. He feared nothing and no one. Tut started to grab the air hoping to touch something

At the same time he spoke.

"What god is this that visits his brother but does not speak?" He reached out and felt Irving's arm and grabbed hold of it. Irving Sussman panicked and pushed at Tut. But Pharaoh had an iron grip and would not let go. Again Irv spoke.

"Mike he's got Me." Things were starting to happen fast and getting out of hand. Mike and Jim both attempted to free Irv from the grip of Pharaoh. Tut realizing that there were at least three gods in his chamber and that they must not be friendly or they wouldn't be hitting and pulling at him. He called for the guards who were at his side in a second. They couldn't see what was hitting and pulling at the young god, but it was evident something was. Pharaoh ordered them to slash at the air around him with their swords. His logic was if he could feel them he could cut them. The two guards, hand-picked by pharaoh for their loyalty, did not hesitate to obey the young gods command. They were raised to believe Pharaoh was a living god and from what they were seeing and hearing, it was obvious to them there were other gods in the room. They were brave men, but Pharaoh had just ordered them to slash at these gods with their swords. They both believed they would die that the gods would kill them for such blasphemies. But they were loyal to pharaoh beyond question. So one of them went to the right of Tut and the other to his left. Jim saw one guard come in his direction, bronze sword held high in the air and coming down with lighting speed. Jim stepped back just as the sword came down missing his chest by inches. The other swung his sword in front of pharaoh; the razor sharp bronze blade met no resistance as it cut through Irving Sussman's shirtsleeve and left arm, severing it just below the elbow. The guard knew instantly he had hit something, because his experience as a warrior and from the scream that the invisible god let out when the sword had hit. Both Pharaoh and the guard upon seeing the blood and hearing the scream renewed with more energy their efforts to subdue these invisible gods.

Tut grabbed for the gold dagger that hung from his belt, still holding onto the arm, Tut struck forward with his knife, plunging it up to the hilt just below Irv's third rib in his left chest. Irv fell to the floor dead. Jim seeing this called out to Mike.

"Mike do something." Janet, seeing what was happening, started to scream. Mike couldn't believe what he was seeing, this shouldn't be happening.

"Sue do something." Both Jim and Mike were shouting at the same time, but when Jim had called out, he stopped for a second, long enough for the second guards gleaming sword to come down on Jim's head. Cleaving it to his chest. Jim was dead before he hit the floor. This guard also knew he had hit something because it fell against him. Janet stopped screaming and was just standing there, shocked and just staring ahead. Now, Tut and the two guards turned their attention toward Mike.

"Sue get me out of here, now." The first guard threw his sword at the voice just as Sue pulled Mike into the future. Now all of this happened in less than sixty seconds. Mike was gone, but Janet was still standing there just behind were Mike was. The guards aim was true and caught Janet in the chest, she fell back dead. Mike couldn't believe what had just happened.

"Holy shit, holy shit, Sue tell me I'm dreaming."

"Tell me this is some kind of trick you're pulling on me, right?"

"No Michael, this is no trick and you are not dreaming."

"How could all this happen? Why didn't you stop it, why did you let it happen?" Mike was yelling.

"Lower your voice or someone will hear you." Mike was shaking

"Where is everyone, where's Jim and Irving and Janet, are they really dead? Where are the bodies, what's going to happen now?" Mike was on the verge of panic.

"I thought we were invisible? How could they see us?"

"They couldn't see you Michael, but they could hear you. You only asked to be invisible, nothing else." Jim and Irving and Janet are dead, I left them in Pharaohs chamber."

"Why did you leave them there? What's going to happen now, I'll be accused of murder."

"Do you want me to bring the three dead bodies back here? If you leave them there, you don't have to get rid of them." Mike was trying to calm down and get a grip on his emotions.

"You will not be accused of murder, because you didn't kill anyone, as to what's going to happen now, I suggest we sit down and plan."

As Sue pulled Mike out of Tut's chamber, Janet, Jim and Irving became visible. The sword thrown by the guard, sailed passed Pharaoh's head and just as Janet became visible. The bodies of the three time travelers lay on the floor before Pharaoh.

Tut had seen people with skin color as pale as these three lying on the floor before him. But he had never seen clothes such as they were wearing. During the excitement, Ankhesenamen had sent one of the servant girls to get more guards. They arrived in time to see the bodies appear out of thin air. Tut turned to the guard that had thrown the sword and said.

"Your sword has found its mark Em-ho-tep, you and Hor-em-set will be rewarded." Both guards fell down on their knees, arms stretched out and head's bowed.

"We only did as you commanded great one."

"You did well, rise, both of you." Tut turned to the guards that just arrived and pointed to two in the rear and commanded them.

"You two in the rear, go fetch the priests that just left here and bring them back."

"We hear and obey." And they turned and ran in the direction of the temple of Isis.

Tut looked down at the three strangers laying dead and pointing to the court yard outside his chambers, said to the remaining guards.

"Bring them outside and strip them, I wish to examine them closer. The guards picked up the three bodies and all the equipment and carried it all out side. They stripped the clothes from the bodies and put them in a pile. Ankhesenamen stepped up and picked up the clothes taken off the female. For the most part, women in Egypt walked around bare breasted. As she examined the bra taken off Janet, she wondered just what purpose it served. She thought to herself that these strangers must have come from the far north were it was cold, this thing must have kept her warm.

Just then the priests arrived and bowed to Pharaoh. Tut pointing at the bodies said to the priests.

"Here priests, look at these strange ones and tell me, are they gods?" the two priests of Isis got off their knees and walked over to the bodies. They poked and probed and felt the bodies, they opened the eyes and moths and examined the teeth. When they got to Janet's body they took a little longer to poke and probe. The two priests examined the clothing and the gear. Then they stepped aside and spoke together in low tones.

"Don't mumble in my presence." Tut shouted.

"Are they gods or not?" The two priests fell to their knees again when Tut shouted.

"Our apologies great one, no, they are not gods."

"Are you sure?"

"Yes my king, gods cannot be killed." Tut was standing and staring at the bodies, he said to them.

"Go, you are dismissed." The two priests bowed and backed out of the chamber, as they left, the commander and chief of Tut's army arrived with twenty men.

"Welcome my friend and general." Tut said

"I came as soon as I heard, great one. I am pleased that you are not hurt my king."

"I'm fine Hor-em-heb, come here my friend perhaps you can tell me who or what these strange visitors are." Tut said pointing to the three naked bodies. Tut related to his general what had happened just minutes ago. Hor-em-heb stepped forward and examined the bodies and their strange equipment.

"No my Pharaoh, I can't tell you who or what they are, but if they appeared as you said, they must be some unknown gods."

"My thoughts exactly, I don't know why the priests can't see that." As they were talking, Tuts wife was examining the Sony tape recorder that Jim had brought along. She pressed the rewind button. The click and noise that came as the tape was rewinding made her jump. Continuing to play with the strange instrument, she pressed the play button. And again the voices were heard. All the guards present drew their swords, not knowing what to expect.

"There, there are the voices again." Tut said looking around before he realized the voices were coming from the box his wife had just dropped in the grass before retreating into the kings chamber with the three servants.

"There must be demons in this box." Tut said standing over the recorder.

"May I try to kill them my king?" Hor-em-heb asked

"Yes general, kill them then take everything here and dump them in the Nile."

"As you wish my king." And Hor-em-heb drew his sword and smashed the tape recorder to pieces."

Then he ordered his men to gather up everything and do as pharaoh commanded. The men took the bodies and all the equipment and carried them to the river. There they commandeered a fishing boat and rowed to the middle of the Nile. Before dumping Janet's body in the river, she was violated by each of the soldiers in the boat.

Meanwhile, back in Jim's office, Mike was thinking. He was finding it hard to get over the tragedy that had befallen the first paid trip to the past. He looked at Sue and said.

"Sue, we have to remove all traces of our ever having been here, we have to go through everything and find any notes Jim may have made about us. We have to find the business card I gave him."

Mike was looking around the room, and his brain was going over what must be done.

"Can you get into the safe over there?" Mike asked, pointing to Jim's safe that stood in one corner of the room.

"Yes."

"Good, let's start there." Mike and Sue walked over to the safe, Sue opened the door like it was never closed. Inside they found the card Mike had given Jim and a diary Jim had started on Mike's visit and the proposed trip back in time. After about forty minutes, they gave up; hoping they had found everything associated with their visit.

"I hope Jim didn't speak to anyone else about us." Mike said

"We might as well go home and try to forget this ever happened."

"Do you want to leave now Michael?"

"Yeah, might as well go, no wait, the treasure, we must take that with us." Mike had almost forgotten the most important part of the visit. They both looked around the room, searching with their eyes for the box he had left the treasure in.

"Where the hell do you think he would put it?" Mike asked no one, just thinking out loud.

"Here it is Michael." Sue said reaching under Jim's desk and pulling the box out.

"Ain't this a bitch." Mike said.

"This shit is priceless, and he puts it under his desk." Mike picked up the money in the envelope and the box and said.

"Before we leave, did you make sure there are no fingerprints of mine anyplace in here?"

"There is nothing here that can point to you Michael, everything is clean as you say."

"Good, let's get out of here before we're seen."

Back in Mike's house, Mike put the box of treasure in the closet in his bedroom, walked into the kitchen and got a beer. He entered the living room and sat down on the sofa. He opened the envelope Jim had put the money in and started to count it.

"Three thousand dollars even, that comes to a thousand a body, I bet murder Inc. got more than that."

"Michael, what happened today was unfortunate, and it's over, we must go on."

Mike looked at Sue, his eyes opened in shock.

"Unfortunate, go on, we were, I mean I was just partner to the murders--."

"No Michael." Sue interrupted him

"You were not partner to nor were you responsible for what happened, it was what your culture calls an accident."

"Yeah, that's easy for you to say, you're not going to spend the rest of your life behind bars."

"Neither are you Michael, let me explain something to you, first all this happened thirty five hundred years ago, all participants are dead. All traces of anything to do with this have vanished. You cannot be accused of murder, the bodies have been disposed of, they were thrown in the Nile for the crocodiles. And again all this happened 3500 yrs ago."

"Wait a minute." Mike broke in.

"How do you know everything was thrown into the Nile?"

"I watched what happened after we left." Mike was puzzled.

"How did you see what happened there when you came back with me?"

"Michael, I have told you several times, there is nothing I can't do."

"Yeah, yeah ok, ok so what happened after we left there?" Sue related to Mike everything that happened after she pulled him out of there.

"You mean they raped Janet in the boat, raped a dead body?"

"Yes Michael, its common practice on your world, in ancient Egypt when a young girl or women died, the family waited a couple of days before taking the body to the embalmers.

"When the body is as you say, a little ripe, they knew the embalmers wouldn't touch it."

"Yeah, I remember reading about that, I guess if your job was embalming, I guess after awhile you kind of stood out in a crowd."

"Yes Michael, in such societies you got your pleasure where you could."

"I guess you're right, from a man's point of view, I guess in their position any man would do the same."

Mike sat back in the chair and slowly finished his beer, then said.

"I'm hungry, let's get something to eat.'

Mike dropped the beer can in the recycle pail and started to walk out the door when a thought hit him. "Sue I've got an idea, I need a partner and I know just who I want. I'm going to call an old friend of mine I haven't seen in years." Mike walked over to the phone and started to dial his old friend DJ that's what everyone called him in the old neighborhood. He dialed the number he remembered and waited.

"Hello?"

"Hello, DJ? I bet you don't know who this is."

"Yeah, you're right, but give me a minute and I'll, hey wait, is this Mike?"

"Yeah, it sure is, how the hell are you, my friend."

"Shit, I'm fine; how the hell are you and where have you been keeping yourself all these years?"

"It's a long story my friend, but that's what I called you about. What are you doing this afternoon DJ?" Mike crossed his fingers and looked at Sue.

"Well, I just washed my car and I thought I'd go get something to eat, why?"

Mike clinched his fist and gave the, all right, sign to Sue.

"You're in luck my friend, how'd you like to go with me to the Star Garden on Steinway St, I'll pay?" the Star garden had been closed for at least 25 years, but Mike wanted to show his old friend what he had in mind.

"Sounds good to me Mike, but don't you remember, that place closed years ago. Where are you Mike?" "I'm home in Jersey, but I'll be there in a flash." Mike hung up the phone and turned to Sue.

"How soon can you get us there Sue?" with the last word spoken, they were standing outside DJ's apt door. "You know Sue, I really wish you'd give me more warning." "It kind of shakes me up." Sue just smiled at Mike. "Sorry Michael, you'll get used to it"

DJ was standing by the phone on the wall when Mike said he was in Jersey. DJ said - cordless phone.

"Mike, there's no way you can get here for lunch, Mike, Mike are you there?" DJ figured the phone went dead when he heard a knock on the door.

"Hold on, I'll be right there." He shook the phone and listened for a noise from the other end, when nothing came through he hung the receiver up and walked over to the door. He was a little disappointed he couldn't finish the conversation with his friend, he hadn't seen Mike in about 5 years, and it would have been a real treat to see him again. DJ opened the door, and his mouth fell open and his eyes widened.

"Mike, how the hell did you." The questions stopped and the two old friends embraced and shook hands smiling and both trying to speak at the same time.

"You got a cell phone right?" DJ asked when the hand shaking stopped.

"No, no cell phone, I called you from my house in Jersey."

"But, but?" DJ was thoroughly confused. Mike patted his old friend on the back and said

"All in good time DJ, now, are you ready to eat?"

"Yeah, I'm ready, but didn't you mention the Star Garden? You know that's been closed for a long time now." DJ spoke the words to Mike but he had his eyes on Sue. Mike saw DJ looking at Sue.

"Oh, I'm sorry DJ, let me introduce my associate, Sue, no last name, Sue, this is My old friend DJ."

Sue put out her hand to shake DJ's hand, but DJ just stood there with his eyes opened wide.

"DJ, this is Sue." DJ suddenly realized he was staring and putting his hand out reached over and shook Sue's hand. "I'm sorry Sue, forgive me for staring, pleased to meet you."

Mike ignored DJ's comment on the Star Garden, and said

"Let's go, I'm starved for some Chinese food. And I haven't been to the Star Garden in years, let's go." Mike pulled DJ towards the door, but DJ stopped.

"Mike, that place is closed, but as long as your buying, let's go."

"Yeah, okay, I'm buying, and we eat at the Garden." As they got closer to the hall, Mike pulled Sue closer and said. "Sue, when we get to the first door, I want you to take us back to 1956, got it?"

"Yes Michael." As they walked out of DJ's apartment, he turned to lock his door and then they continued on down the hall. As they got to the door, DJ stopped and looked a little confused.

"What's the matter DJ?" Mike said watching the confusion spread over his friend's face.

"I'm not sure, but I have this strange feeling this hall is different than it was before, but I can't pinpoint anything." Mike took his old friend by the shoulder and led him outside. Mike had a smile on his face that was getting bigger by the second. When they got outside on the street DJ stopped and looked around, his confusing was getting deeper.

"Holy shit, Mike someone stole my car, it was right there." DJ was pointing to a spot now occupied by a 1952 Ford. "I've got to call the police." And DJ turned to reenter his apartment building he stopped and gave the building a once over.

"What's wrong DJ?" Mike asked watching the confusion take over his friend completely.

"Mike, what's going on here, there's something strange happening here, I don't know what, but something is definitely wrong." Mike pulled his friend arm and started to walk down the street.

"Come on DJ, let me explain, forget about your car, it hasn't gone anyplace." DJ turned to Mike and attempting to pull away and go make the phone call to the police.

"What do you mean, it's still there, I know where I parked it this morning and it's gone."

"Trust me with this one DJ and just walk with me to the corner and I'll straighten everything out for you." DJ was still in a fog as to what was happening, and the confusion that had taken over his mind was getting still deeper. As they walked to the corner, DJ was looking around the street he had lived on for the past year, and all he was seeing was old cars. Cars from the fifties, old Chevy's and Fords. He saw Ramblers and there was a Hudson. There wasn't one new car on the block. Even the buildings looked different. As they approached the corner were his street met 30th Ave. they stopped.

"Okay DJ, now does anything else look strange to you?" Mike asked, motioning with his arm in a circle for his friend to look all around. DJ stood there turning around and looking at everything.

"Mike I don't know what's going on here, do you want to explain to me what's happening?"

"Okay, okay, let me straighten you out before you blow a gasket in your brain." Mike took his friend by the shoulders and looking him right in the eyes, said to him.

"DJ, we are back in the year 1956," DJ looked at his friend and said "1956? Yeah, right." But then DJ started to think; he took another look around and then back to Mike.

"Mike, what the hell have you been doing these past five years, how the hell did you do this."

DJ finely realized that Mike was right, the proof was right before him, and he started to smile when the reality finely struck him. "Holy shit, this is really 1956, my god Mike, how did you do it?" A million questions were forming in his mind and he didn't know where to start first. There was a little candy store on the corner in 1956 that wasn't there anymore, he turned to the store and walked over and picked up the "Daily Mirror", "Look Mike, the Daily Mirror, I used to love this paper when I was a kid."

Mike was starting to get caught up in the excitement of the moment and pulled DJ away from the candy store and said. "Come on my friend, let's take a walk down Steinway Street." Mike and DJ both forgot about food for awhile

As the three time travelers walked down the street, they were pointing out stores they haven't seen in years. "Look DJ, Lascalzo's, my mother used to buy all her appliances there."

"Hey Mike, let's take a look inside Socals, I used to love that place."

Mike and DJ and Sue, walked and up and down the street, pointing to stores and people they remembered from their youth. Memories popping up that had long lain dormant in the backs of their minds. People turned and looked at the trio as they laughed and generally acted like little kids instead of the adults they were supposed to be. As they approached the "Boys and Men's" store, they stopped.

"Hey Mike, get a look at this, do you remember these?" DJ said pointing to a pair of Chino pants in the window. "Look DJ, they got a belt in the back." The two friends were standing close to the window when DJ spoke. "Man, I've got to get me some of those. Come on, let's go inside and pick up some."

"Okay, I'm game, let's go." So into the store the three went, as they entered the store the sales clerk came up to them. "Good afternoon, can I help you?" DJ said.

"Yeah, I'd like to buy a couple of pair of those chino's you have in the window."

"Ok, would you come over here and I'll measure you." DJ followed the salesmen to one side and Mike and Sue were looking at the shirts, Mike wasn't really interested in buying, he just wanted to check out the prices. "Hey Sue, look at this." Mike picked up a Van Husen shirt and pointed to the price, $2.50.

"This same shirt in 2012 costs about $60.00 at least." DJ picked out 6 pair of chinos in his size and took them to the cash register. The lady behind the counter rang up the pants and said.

"That will be $30.00 please." DJ opened his wallet and took out a fifty-dollar bill and handed it to the lady. "What's this?" the women asked looking at the money DJ had just handed her.

"I can't except this." She said and handed the money back. DJ looked at the women and then at Mike.

It hit Mike like a hammer. The bill DJ had given the women was a newly designed fifty dollar-bill.

Mike thought fast. "Here DJ, let me pay for this." And handing the women thirty dollars that he had in his wallet, money he had asked Sue to change into currency of the year 1956. The women behind the counter took Mikes money, but she looked at DJ and said.

"What kind of money was that?" Mike answered

"That was some stage money we had made up for a movie we're making in a week or so." Pointing to DJ, Mike said to the women. "He took some with him to take to a local printer, we're trying to have some more printed up." That seemed to placate her suspicions, she packed up the pants in a bag and handed them to DJ. The three time travelers left the store, outside on the street Mike said to Sue. "Sue, change his money to current year. DJ, I had my money changed before we left your house, I should have remembered about your money. I was going to treat you to lunch, so the thought never crossed my mind."

"Yeah, I know what you mean. Now I'm getting hungry, let's go eat." They continued their walk down memory lane in the direction of the restaurant. When they got to the Star Garden they stopped outside.

"Man, I thought I'd never see this place again Mike, come on, let's go in."

They entered the restaurant. The owner walked up to them and smiled, he asked

"A table for three?"

"Yeah, and could you make it a booth we'd like some privacy." Mike asked.

"Certainly, this way please." They followed the man to a booth in the rear of the restaurant and were seated. The waiter came over and gave them menus and set the table up for three. He left and walked into the kitchen, letting the three decide what they wanted. Mike turned to Sue and said.

"We're gonna need some privacy, could you like make this booth sound proof, so no one can hear what's being said?" Sue looked at Mike and said.

"Anything else you want Michael?" Mike looked at DJ and again to Sue.

"Yeah, could you make the booth sound proof?"

"I already did Michael." "Oh yeah, I forgot, you do things at light speed." He turned to DJ, but DJ spoke first. "I notice that every time you want something you ask Sue here."

"That's what I want to talk to you about." Just as Mike started to talk, the waiter returned.

"Would you like a drink before you order?"

"Yeah, what kind of beer do you have?" DJ asked.

"Rheingold, Schaffer and Ballantine." The waiter replied

"I'll have a scotch on the rocks." Mike said.

DJ said, "I'll have a Beer." "Nothing for the lady." Mike said. Sue turned to the waiter.

"I'll have a scotch on the rocks also." The waiter bowed and turned to leave, he was writing on his pad and stopped about 6 feet from the booth, he turned around and addressed DJ.

"What kind of beer would you like sir?" DJ replied "Ballantine." Now the waiter saw DJ's mouth move, but nothing came out of it. So again he asked.

"Sir, what kind of beer would you like?" and again DJ said. "Ballantine." Now the waiter thought that the man in the booth was making fun of him, so he turned and stormed off.

"What bit him?" DJ asked.

"You got me." Mike replied.

"He couldn't hear you because of the sound barrier you asked for." Sue said. Mike hit himself on the forehead. "Shit I forgot. Listen, DJ, when we make trips in time, we'll have to make sure we cover every little detail." "I've already made one big mistake today, I don't want to make another."

DJ was looking a little confused, he asked. "What do you mean you made one big mistake today?"

Just then, the waiter and the owner walked out of the kitchen and approached the table. He motioned for the waiter to wait, and he came over to the booth alone.

"Is everything alright gentlemen?"

"Everything is just fine so far." Mike replied "Why do you ask?"

"My waiter said you sir." He said pointing at DJ. "Were making fun of him."

"Me, I don't even know the man, why would I do that?"

DJ continued. "If he took offence at anything I said, bring him over here and I'll apologize."

"Believe me I meant no harm." Mr. ye, the owner of the Star Garden, looked at the three customers sitting before him, and satisfied with DJ's explanation, said.

"That won't be necessary, I can see it was all a mistake. Enjoy your meals." He turned and walked away; he stopped by the waiter said something to him in Chinese and went to the back of the restaurant. The waiter came back to the table and again asked DJ what kind of beer he wanted.

"Ballantine." DJ stood up and taking the waiters hand said

"Please except my apology my friend, I didn't mean to offend you in any way."

The waiter was appeased, shook DJ's hand and returned to the bar to get the drinks.

"Very diplomatic." Mike said, "You handled that very well."

"You know I like to avoid confrontations at all costs, I'm not a fighter, I'm a lover."

"Speak for yourself." Mike said. "I've been dabbling in the martial arts for the past three years."

"I can handle myself better now than I could when I was 35yrs old."

"Sure you can." DJ said scoffing.

"Tell him Sue." Mike said. "He's right DJ, he's used it a couple of times already today." Sue was referring to the incident in the school.

"Well I'll be damned, you got to show me some of those moves."

"Sure thing, as soon as we get the chance, but first let me tell you what's going on."

"You've got my whole attention, I've been waiting for this."

As Mike started to tell DJ the whole story, the waiter returned with the drinks. As he was placing them on the table, DJ's watch started to beep. The waiter stopped and looked at the watch.

"That noise, its coming from your watch?" He asked as DJ reached over with his right hand to turn it off. Keeping the watch covered he said "Yeah, it's just to remind me I got to do something."

The waiter kept looking at watch and said to DJ.

"Your watch made a noise, I never heard a watch make a noise before."

"It's just something I rigged up myself." The waiter had gotten a look at the watch before it was covered up. He noticed that it was something he had never seen before, it had no hands, only what looked like square numbers, and there was a lot of small buttons beneath the numbers.

To break up what he thought was going to blow up, Mike said

"We'd like to order now." The waiter turned his attention from the watch to his job, took the orders and returned to the kitchen gave the orders to the cook and went out to see the owner.

Mr. Ye was sitting at a little table reserved for himself, it was in a strategic position where he could keep an eye on things. The waiter approached the table and bowed.

"Excuse me Mr. Ye, I don't want to seem like a complainer, but it's those three people I told you about before." "Yes Tommy what is it?" Mr. Ye spoke without taking his eyes off the table were Mike and DJ and Sue sat. "May I tell you what I observed?"

"Yes Tommy, please do."

"Well Mr. Ye, the one I told you about before, the one who didn't speak, he has a watch like no watch I've ever seen before." "Mr. Ye looked at his waiter.

"What about the watch Tommy?"

"It's different, it has no hands, it has buttons and it makes a noise."

"What kind of noise did it make?"

"It sounded like eeep, eeep, eeep. When I asked him what it was, he said it was just something he made to remind him." Mr. Ye again turned his attention to the three in the booth and said.

"Thank you for you observation Tommy, I'll look into it."

The waiter bowed and returned to the kitchen. Mr. Ye remembered when he was speaking to the trio before, he noticed the watch on the man's arm, he had gotten a good look at it from less than six feet away. His family owned a watch factory in Hong Kong that made cheap watches for Europe and America. He and his brother studied watch making and repair in Switzerland, he had seen nothing like that watch before.

The food was delivered, while they all ate, Mike was telling his old friend everything. They were renewing and old friendship and it felt like old times again. Mike turned to Sue.

"Sue would you mind if DJ and I spent the rest of the day together, you know like just walking around like we did when we were kids. We have a lot to catch up on, and now that we're going to be partners, we have a lot to discuss."

"Okay Michael, I'll keep in touch the old way."

"Thanks Sue, and don't get lost."

"As you would say Michael, when you need me I'll be here in a heartbeat."

"It's a comfort knowing you're so close." Mike said the last with tongue in cheek, Sue knew he was referring to the little episode in Tut's chambers. Which he was just going to tell DJ about. DJ busy eating looked up just in time to see Sue vanish. DJ's mouth fell open.

"Where'd she go?"

"I told her we were going to spend the day just walking around like we used to do when we were kids, that we had a lot to discuss now that we were going to be partners. Don't worry, if we need her, Sue will be here in a heartbeat.

Across the room, Mr. Ye saw the girl disappear. At first he thought she'd slipped beneath the table, but when the other two didn't react, he decided to get a closer look. The more the owner thought about the party in the rear booth, the more he was convinced there was something very odd about them. Mr. Ye was known to get up and walk around visiting the tables and asking if everything was okay. He got up and started his little tour of the restaurant in a clockwise direction. Stopping now and then to either talk to a customer or pretend to arrange a place setting on the unoccupied tables. Mike and DJ were unaware of his approach. Mr. Ye stopped at the table in the booth next to were the two time travelers were sitting. He sensed there was something different something odd that at first he couldn't quite put his finger on. A customer at a table on the other side of the room dropped his fork, then what was wrong hit Mr. Ye, there was no sound coming from the booth next to him. He could hear what was going on in all the booths and tables were someone was sitting. But from the booth next to him, nothing, only silence.

In the booth, Mike had just finished his story. DJ knew it was the truth, he was sitting in the Star Garden in 1956. DJ asked Mike.

"Do you still have the treasure from Tut's tomb?"

"Yeah, its home in the closet." DJ had stopped eating and was contemplating all Mike was saying to him. He was very interested in this time travel thing. But even though he knew it was real, it had come up so suddenly, his mind was spinning trying to sort everything out. DJ looked at Mike.

"And you want me in on this, to be your partner?"

"Yeah, remember when we were teenagers? We were always close, we think alike. Besides I couldn't think of anybody I'd rather have as a partner." A big smile crossed DJ's face.

"Okay, I'm in." they shook hands. And DJ reached into his wallet and pulled out one of those small pocked calculators.

"Let's see, gold is going for about $350.00 an ounce." Mike cut in

"Wait a minute, I'm not selling the treasure DJ."

"Yeah I know, but there's got to be a lot of gold out there somewhere in the past waiting to be picked up and taken home. I mean we got to have some operating cash and money to live on."

"Yeah, your right DJ, I'm still new at this, and with your devious mind, we should be able to make a small fortune to live on." DJ put the calculator down and looked at his friend.

"Look, Mike I know a lot about coins, we could make a small fortune picking up some real rare or no longer available coins and selling them to the right people."

"That's a good idea, yeah I like that." Before DJ could continue with this line of thought, Mr. Ye was standing by their table.

"Hello again gentlemen, I hope you enjoyed your meals?"

"Yes." Mike said, "Everything was very good." Mr. Ye looked at the spot where Sue was sitting.

"Where's the young lady?"

"She went to the lady's room." Mike said. Mr. Ye turned around and spoke in Chinese to the young lady at the register. Then turned back to Mike and DJ and said.

"I don't think so." Mike and DJ looked at each other and Mike spoke.

"What do you mean, you don't think so, are you calling me a liar?" Mr. Ye turned to the young lady standing by the lady's room door and nodded, the girl walked into the room and after a couple of second's came out and shook her head no.

Mr. Ye pointed to the seat next to Mike and said

"My I?" He sat down without waiting for a reply from Mike.

"Allow me to be blunt, there's something strange about you two and I'm going to find out just what it is." Mike turned in his seat so he was kind of facing Mr. Ye.

"Are you now." DJ looked at Mike, he was getting a little nervous. "May be we should leave Mike?" Mr. Ye waved his hand and the kitchen door opened and out came three of his kitchen helpers. "No Gentlemen, please don't try to leave, just yet. You see my waiter, Tommy, came over to tell me about the watch you are wearing." The owner said pointing to the DJ's wrist. DJ started to say something but Mr. Ye put up his hand and stopped him.

"Let me finish, please. You see just after Tommy finished telling me what he had observed and walked away, I saw the young lady that was sitting here disappear."

"Yeah, like I told you she went to the bathroom." Mike said.

"No no my young friend, I don't mean she got up and walked away, I mean she disappeared, vanished from sight." DJ was starting to sweat. Just about then the waiter and the two men from the kitchen stopped at the table. Mr. Ye smiled at the men and pointing at them said to Mike.

"Gentlemen, I would like you to meet Mr. Young." The man the owner was pointing at was a student of karate like Mike and was used now and then to remove from the restaurant unruly customers. Mr. Ye continued. "He's shall we say, the house bouncer." Mike was very calm and turned to DJ and said. "Well well what do you know, we're being threatened." Now DJ was really starting to get worried. Mike looked at Mr. Ye and said. "Just what is your name, I'm going to need it for the police report." "It is not necessary that you know my name, again let me be blunt." Mr. Ye related to Mike and DJ all he had observed since they arrived in his restaurant. He told them how he stood next to their booth but heard no noise come from it even though they were talking. Mike remembered the sound barrier he had asked Sue to put up around the booth and said to himself that the next time he has got to be more careful. Mr. Ye finished. Mike looked at him and said.

"So?" "So before I let you leave, I want the watch and I want you to tell me how it works?

DJ started to remove the watch he was visibly shaken. While Mr. Ye was talking, Mike was communicating with Sue. He told her to remove the barrier from the booth and when the time was right, she should come out of the lady's room and come over to the booth.

"No DJ, put the watch back on. Now I've got a proposition for you. When my girlfriend comes out of the bathroom, you." He said pointing at Mr. Ye. "You will not only apologize for this insult, but you will pay for the meal. And now." Mike said pointing to the man from the kitchen.

"Call off Bruce Lee here before he gets hurt and I'll forget about going to the police. And if you don't, after I finish with Bruce here, I'll not only have the cops on you but the board of health too."

Mr. Ye smiled and stood up, he was about to tell his bouncer to do his work, when he noticed Sue walk out of the lady's room and walk over to the booth. He couldn't believe what he was looking at. He pointed to Sue and said something to the girl at the register in Chinese. When Sue got over to the booth she said. "What's up Mike?"

"Nothing Sue, the owner here just bought us lunch, come on DJ, let's go." They stood up to go. Mr. Ye was very shaken up, he looked at Sue and asked.

"Where did you come from, I saw you disappear?" Sue played her part very well.

"I came from the lady's room, where did you think I came from?" She turned to Mike.

"Is there something going on here I don't know about?"

"Nah, it's all over now, come on lets go." As Mike and DJ started to leave the booth, the man from the kitchen stepped in front of Mike. Pointing to the bouncer Mike asked the owner.'

"Do you want to call off Bruce here before he gets hurt, or do you want a scene and a lot of damage to your place?" Mr. Ye was not paying much attention to the situation, he was mumbling to himself in Chinese and he waved his hand at the bouncer to let them pass. While this was happening, Mike was speaking to Sue in his mind, he told her to change DJ's watch to a cheap Timex watch of the fifties. Mike turned to DJ and said.

"DJ, why don't you give the gentlemen your watch, it will be a cheap watch for a cheap meal. DJ started to remove the watch from his wrist and when he looked at the watch, his mouth fell open. As they started to pass the bouncer the man gave Mike a little shove. He figured he'd put a little fear in these round eyes, and show them how bad he was, he liked to see the fear in people's eyes. Mike was pushed about three feet. He turned to look at the man. Mike was pissed. The man was standing arms crossed and smiling.

Mike was mad as hell and he reacted faster then he thought he could, he gave the bouncer a spinning back kick right to the stomach and sent him crashing over a table. He landed on the floor doubled over and very hurt. The owner of the Star Garden was holding the cheap watch DJ had handed him. He was more confused than ever. Mike handed the waiter a five-dollar bill and said to him.

"Here, your boss is paying for the meal, there's no reason you should miss out on a tip.

They left the restaurant and walked north along Steinway St. DJ spoke first.

"Mike I got to say I'm very impressed with your karate, you have to show me that stuff if we're going to be partners." Mike stopped and faced DJ.

"Any time you're ready, we'll go to my house and make plans for some travels and I'll show you a few moves."

"Michael do you want me to go?"

"Yeah, but this time could you like take a walk around the corner and disappear rather than just vanishing in front of everybody?"

"Okay Michael." Sue turned and walked to the corner, rounded it and vanished.

Mike and DJ continued their walk up memory lane. Stopping and pointing at things that were no more. DJ was having so much fun; he started to worry about time.

"Mike how much time do we have left to spend back here?"

"We have all the time we want DJ, all the time we want."

"Great, I got an idea, why don't we take a cab around the neighborhood and like site see."

"Hey, that's a good idea DJ. Just in case we meet someone who might get a little suspicious as to who we are, know what I mean?" "Yeah you're right, here comes one now, hey man look, it's one of those Desoto's with the open roof." DJ stepped off the curb and hailed the cab. The yellow and green Desoto pulled over and Mike and DJ got in. Mike asked the cabby if he would mind just cruising around the area, he explained that they were from around here but had moved away and just wanted to look the old place over. The driver said it was all right with him as long as they paid the meter. So off they went. DJ told the driver where to start the tour. They wanted to ride down Steinway St. and when they got to Broadway he should make a left turn and go slowly.

As they were riding they were looking this way and that, like a couple of kids in a toy store. DJ asked. "Hey Mike, what do we do if we see ourselves?" Mike didn't know what to say, he just shrugged. The driver heard the conversation, but pushed it to the back of his mind. Mike turned to DJ. "Remember what I told you in the restaurant, I was already inside my younger self. Seeing ourselves, well it should be like seeing a movie I guess." DJ thought for a second.

"Yeah I guess you're right, but I hope we don't find out." The cab driver made a left turn and then another and yet a third to get them in the direction they wanted to go. As they turned onto Steinway St again, DJ said. "Hey man look, Lofts candy, I almost forgot what it looked like, that place burned down in the late sixties didn't it?"

"Yeah, I think it was around 67 or 68. Hey DJ, look, Tom McAnn shoes, maybe we should stop by later and check out the prices, maybe pick up couple of pairs."

"Yeah, you don't see prices like that anymore. Hey check out the school, didn't they tare down that place around 65?" Mike looked at the old school house and said.

"I can remember them knocking it down, what a shame, torn down to make a parking lot."

DJ added "And remember, they put up that kookie kingdom place."

"Oh yeah I forgot." The driver was listening to the conversation his two riders were having, but he couldn't make any sense out of it. Lofts burned down, the school torn down. These two were talking as if these events already happened. Again he pushed the conversation to the back of his mind.

When they got to Broadway, the driver made a left turn as instructed. Mike tapped the driver on the shoulder and told him. "When you get to 48th St. make a right and go slower.

"What ever you say Mac." They drove about a block when Mike grabbed DJ's arm.

"Holy shit DJ look."

"Where?"

"There." Mike was pointing at a woman walking with a little girl.

"Its Carol. Driver go another block and pull over to the curb."

"You gotten out Mac?"

"No, I just want to watch for a minute." As the women and the little girl approached, Mike became mesmerized. "That's my girlfriend."

Mike was sitting on the edge of the seat trying to get a better look.

"DJ, I'm in love again." The driver turned around to see who Mike was talking about.

"That women is your girlfriend?" He asked

"No not the women, the blonde girl with the pony tail." The cabbies eye's widened a little. DJ noticed what was going on and he nudged Mike in the ribs. The cabby said to Mike

"The little girls your girlfriend?" all of sudden Mike realized what he was saying and trying to get himself out of it said. "I mean she was my, er, will be my, never mind I must have made a mistake."

"Do you want to continue?" the driver asked

"No, just another minute." Mike kept his eyes on the little girl who would someday capture his heart all over again. "Let's go." DJ said "We're finished here." As they pulled away, Mike turned his head to watch the women and the little girl disappear. The cabby couldn't put his finger on it, but there was something very strange about the pair in the back of his cab. At 46 St. they caught the light.

"Hey look DJ, Mike said pointing out the window. "Those two lots, remember?"

"Yeah, on that one they built a diner and this one over here is where they put up the Salvation Army building." Something caught DJ's eye.

"Hey Mike, look, my fathers car." DJ was pointing out the front window to a little blue two door 46 Plymouth that his father drove for years. He started to get out of the cab.

"I've got to talk to him." Mike restrained his friend.

"No DJ you can't, he wont know who you are, your older then you were in 1956." The driver was listening and trying to remember everything that was being said.

"He don't have to know its Me."

"No DJ, you can't, you might say something that would change history or something."

"Try to understand DJ, we're not here to interfere or change anything, we're only visiting."

"Listen my friend, how do you think I'd feel if I saw my mother walking along the street, don't you think I'd like to give her a hug and a kiss? Of course I would, but she wouldn't know me and would probably scream and run away or have me arrested." DJ still looking at the blue car in front of them said. "Yeah, I guess you're right."

"Hey Mac." The driver called from the front seat. "I know I shouldn't be listening to your conversation but I couldn't help it." The light changed and the driver pulled over and stopped at the curb.

"But why wouldn't his father know him and why would your mother scream and run away? And how can he be older then he was in 1956, this IS 1956?" Mike thought to himself "I did it again."

He figured he had nothing to lose at this point and besides they wouldn't be here much longer. So he said. "Well for one thing, we are 40 years older then we were in 1956, because we just dropped in from 2012 for a visit." The driver looked at Mike and smiled.

"Sure you are." Mike motioned for him to continue the driver turned back to his driving but told himself that he had to remember as much as he could about these two. As they drove away from the curb,

Mike poked DJ and said. "Hey look, John's barber shop, and there's John, oh man this is great."

The driver couldn't concentrate on his driving and listen to these two, so he pulled over again to the curb. "What's the matter driver?" Mike asked.

"You're pulling my leg about being from the future, right? I mean time travel isn't possible right?"

"Look, I really don't have the time to explain right now but" And just then DJ says

"Hey Mike, look, Bohacks, what say we get out here and do a little shopping? And besides I think we're missing to much by riding and I don't think anyone would really know who we are."

"Yeah, I guess you're right." Mike pulls out a hundred dollar bill and hands it to the driver.

"Hey Mac, I don't have change of that."

"That's all right, you keep the change." Mike and DJ got out of the cab.

After the three travelers left the restaurant, they stood on the sidewalk and talked for a minute. Inside the restaurant, Tommy helped the injured man up and together with other help from the kitchen they straightened out the mess left from the short fight. Tommy started to clean off the table were Mike and DJ had sat. He picked up the napkin DJ was using and found the pocket calculator DJ had left there. The waiter called to Mr. Ye, look, they left something." Mr. Ye walked over and took the object Tommy held out for him. Forgetting the watch, Mr. Ye noticed this strange thing had small rubber pads, over each was a number from 1 to 0. And there was a box with square zeros in it. He walked over to a light hanging from the ceiling to get a better look. The square zeros got darker under the light. "I've got them now." He said to him self. He called into the kitchen for another man. Charlie Wong came out and walked over to his boss. Charlie had come from Hong Kong with Mr. Ye, he had worked for the family 10 years, he was a loyal employee. In China, Charlie was a long distance runner.

Mr. Ye spoke to Charlie in Chinese telling him what had happened so far this afternoon. Then he showed him what was left behind, he handed him some money and told Charlie to follow the trio and report back by phone when he could. When Mike and DJ got into the cab, Charlie had no difficulty keeping up with them because of traffic.

When the cab pulled over to the curb at 47th St. and the two passengers got out, Charlie slipped into the cab from the other door.

"Where to Mac?" The driver asked.

"Don't go anywhere, I want to speak to you." Charlie watched as Mike and DJ entered the supermarket. "Tell me about those two." He said pointing in the direction of Mike and DJ.

"Those two? What about them?"

"Tell me all you know, they were in my store acting very strangely."

"Yeah, their a couple of strange birds, but listen Mac, if you want to talk, I'll have to put the flag down, time is money you know." Charlie handed him a twenty dollar bill and said

"Tell me what you know."

"Well, when they got into my cab on Steinway St. they started to talk about the stores, certain stores like they were surprised they were still standing. Like loft candy, they said it burned down in the late 60's and the school, they said it was torn down in the early 60's. You know, like those things already happened."

"What else?" Charlie asked. The cabby related to the man in his back seat everything else he could remember about the strange pair. Meanwhile, inside the market, Mike and DJ were having a ball walking around the isles comparing prices and finding brands that no longer existed. DJ picked up a bag full of groceries, things he hadn't had in years, he paid for them and they left the market.

"Will you wait here for me?" Charlie asked the driver handing him another twenty dollar bill."

"Sure thing pal." He thought to himself "I haven't made this much money since I found the diamond ring in the back seat last year."

Charlie got out of the car and walked over to the market. He positioned himself just outside the exit door. He only waited about a minute when they walked out. He stepped in front of them.

"Can I help you?" Mike asked

"No, but my employer has something that belongs to you and he would like to return it."

"What does he have that belongs to us?" Mike asked

"That's just it, he doesn't know what it is, he would like you to come back to the restaurant and explain it to him."

"I don't think your boss has anything that belongs to us." And he turned to walk away.

"Wait Mike." DJ said

"What?"

"I think I know what he has."

"Yeah, what?"

"Remember we were talking about the gold?"

They both said it at the same time.

"The calculator."

"I'm sorry Mike, everything happened so fast, I forgot."

"That's alright DJ, we just have to plan things a little better the next trip."

Mike took DJ by the elbow and pulled him away so Charlie couldn't hear what he was going to say. "This may be a trap, but it's okay." DJ looked from Mike to Charlie and back to Mike.

"You mean Sue?"

"Yeah, Sue. Okay my friend lead the way." Mike said to Charlie. Charlie smiled his boss Mr. Ye would be very happy. "This way please." Charlie said, motioning them towards the waiting cab.

"Hey DJ, look, our cab." DJ stopped Mike and said. "I'd like to drop these groceries off at my place first, carrying them around, you know, they'll just get in the way."

"I'll take care of everything." Mike was beginning to feel a serge of power he never felt before, and he didn't care who saw what was going on. Again he whispered to DJ.

"Sue is aware of everything that's going on." They got into the taxi along with Charlie.

"The Star Garden on Steinway St." Charlie said to the driver."

"You remember the place where you picked us up from." Mike said

"Oh yeah." "But first, I would like you to drive down 41st St. from 28th Ave. so my friend here can drop off this bag first."

"Okay Mac." Charlie started to protest. "We must go to the restaurant first."

"Don't worry." Mike said. "It's only around the corner from the restaurant and it will only take a minute." Mike was talking to Sue in his mind. He was telling her that as soon as they got to the corner of 41st and 28th Ave. she was to bring them to 2012 so DJ could put the groceries in his apartment. And that when they drove down to 30th Ave. she was to bring them back to 1956. And he instructed her to return to the bathroom in the restaurant and to emerge at the proper time. Sue said she understood and that everything would go as planned.

"DJ as soon as we finish with the restaurant, we'll go to my house and make some plans."

"Sounds good to me Mike." As they rode through the streets they were pointing to places that they hadn't seen in years. Old friends they had forgotten or hadn't seen in years. As the car approached 41ˢᵗ St and 28ᵗʰ Ave. Mike poked DJ in the ribs. DJ figured something was going to happen but he wasn't quite sure what. As the Desoto started to turn into 41ˢᵗ St. things started to change. The driver noticed it first. "What the?" now Charlie was beginning to notice things also.

"What's going on here?" the driver asked. Mike and DJ started to smile.

"What do you mean?"

"Look at these car's, did you ever see anything like them before?" the driver was trying to look at these strange car's and drive at the same time.

"Sure I have, these are all models from the eighties and nineties."

"Eighties and nineties?" Mike was really enjoying this.

"Pull up to that apartment house over there." The driver slowed down and stopped where DJ had pointed. Charlie and the driver couldn't figure out what was going on, but both were convinced something very strange just happened.

DJ got out of the cab and carried his bag of groceries into his apartment. Mike just sat back in the cab and watched the other two try to figure out just what was going on. The driver couldn't take his eyes off the cars. And Charlie was taking mental notes of everything he saw.

As they waited for DJ to emerge from the building, two men in their fifties were approaching for the direction the cab was facing. The taller one poked the other and said.

"Hey, check out the old cab. Man I haven't seen one like that in what, forty years?"

"Yeah, and its in pretty good shape for being that old." The other man said. They walked over the cab and the taller one put his face in the side window.

"Hey Mac, this you're cab?" With much effort, the driver took his eyes off the cars around him and answered. "No it belongs to the Manhattan Cab co." The other man said.

"Oh yeah right, their making a movie and this guys playing the role to the hilt." The two craned their necks and looked around for the cameras.

The taller one said. "I don't see anything, must be down the next street." He looked into the cab again and asked. "Who's making the movie, MGM, Paramount?" Just then DJ came out of the house and approached the cab to get in.

"Excuse me." He said, trying to get into the cab.

"Hey, I know you." The smaller man said pointing to DJ. "Your, eh your, hell I can't think of your name but I've seen you on television." Now the other man joined in.

"Yeah, your right, I can't think of his name ether." DJ climbed into the cab.

"Okay driver, let's go." DJ said.

As they pulled away the two men were trying to remember who DJ was. Seeing the cab pull away, they ran after it, wanting to get another look at the TV star they just saw. Inside the cab, Charlie was taking in all he saw, Mr. Ye would be very interested in what was going on here.

A sign tacked to a tree caught Charlie's attention. It read. "Multi-family tag sale in St. Joseph's school yard, Saturday, July 12, 1998." As the car approached the corner of 30th Ave. and turned, it vanished. The two men chasing the car stopped in their tracks, not believing what they just saw they ran to the corner and looked for the Desoto, but it was gone.

"Hey Mac, what happened back there?" The driver asked, looking at Mike in the rear view mirror. "What do ya mean?" Mike asked smiling.

"You know what I mean, those cars, I never saw cars like that before, where did they come from?"

"Probably Detroit." Mike said. Charlie kept the sign to himself; there was definitely something strange about these two people. His boss would like to hear what Charlie had seen so far.

The cab pulled up in front of the Chinese restaurant and Mike and DJ got out. Charlie paid for the ride and asked the driver if he would park the car and return to the restaurant. The driver said he would be glad to do it if he could just find out what the hell was going on around here.

They entered the restaurant and were greeted by the owner.

"Thank you for returning gentlemen, I hope there are no bad feelings left from our first meeting?"

"None what so ever." Mike said and motioned for DJ to sit with him at a table.

Charlie and Mr. Ye stood near and talked in Chinese. Mr. Ye was told all that had happened since Charlie left in pursuit of these two. He told His boss about the driver, who had just entered the restaurant. The owner found the part about what had happened around the corner very interesting. He told Charlie to make a quick check around the block to see if anything had changed. Then he spoke with the cab driver for about five minutes. The driver told him everything that had happened to him since those two strangers had entered his cab. The owner thanked him and offered to buy him lunch, the driver excepted and sat down.

Now Mr. Ye turned to Mike and DJ.

"Hello again gentlemen."

"Hi, I hope you didn't bring us back here to pay the bill?" Mike asked, making conversation.

"No, no, nothing like that." Mr. Ye said as he sat down. He motioned with his hand and three men stepped out of the shadows. One of them was the man Mike had the run in with earlier. Mr. Young walked over and stood right in front of Mike, he looked right into Mike's eyes and cracked his knuckles. Mike looked back at him and smiled.

The owner pulled DJ's calculator out of his pocket and placed it on the table.

He looked at Mike and DJ and said.

"I'm not sure what this is, but I know the technology to create it doesn't exist yet. Do you want to tell me what it is and how it works?" Mr. Ye was looking from Mike to DJ, and DJ was beginning to get nervous with the three men standing by the table.

"Go on DJ, tell the man how it works." Mike said poking his friend in the shoulder.

"Well er, I er, well you see it." DJ was too nervous to get the words out.

"Okay, let me show you." Mike picked up the calculator and turned it around so Mr. Ye could see it. "Listen, before I start to explain this thing to you, could you arrange for some tea, I've always liked the tea you serve in these restaurant's."

Mr. Ye made a slight motion with his head, keeping his eyes on Mike and DJ.

One of the waiters nearby went into the kitchen and returned with a pot of tea and three cups. The waiter poured the tea and stepped back. Mike began.

"You see, this is what we call a pocket calculator, an adding machine, but it does more than just add up numbers." The owner was becoming engrossed. "Where does it get its power from?"

"It gets its power from light, any light."

"But were are the moving parts, is there more to it then just this piece?"

"It has no moving parts and this is all there is to it." Mr. Ye took the strange thing from Mike's hand and started playing with it. He thought to himself "It gets its power from light, that explains why the square zero's got darker when I brought it into the light."

"Where did you get it from?" The owner asked. Mike poured some more tea into the three cups, filling them to the brim. As he was doing this he looked over at DJ and winked.

"My friend here." Mike said pointing to DJ. "Bought it in the drug store on the corner."

Mr. Ye looked at one of the three men standing around the table and said something in Chinese.

The man ran out the door and down the street. Mike had been talking to Sue in his mind and he asked her if she could let DJ know just what he had in mind.

"Yes Michael, I can do it. DJ has been informed as to your plans." Mike turned to Mr. Ye and said "No no, you won't find it at the corner for another, what, maybe thirty years yet. You sent your man off on a wild goose chase." The owner looked at Mike and wrinkled his brow.

"You said it yourself." Mike said to Mr. Ye. "Remember you said that the technology for this doesn't exist yet? Well you're right. Now the owner was really confused, he looked up at the three remaining men standing around the table and spoke to them in Chinese. Mike looked over at DJ and winked, it was time to act and get out of here.

Mike picked up his cup of tea and tossed it into the face of one man standing by the table, DJ did the same to one of the men closest to him. The scalding hot tea was just the diversion they needed. It caught everyone by surprise, Mike picked his end of the table up and knocked it over on the owner, and with the same movement, hit the man he called, Bruce, in the chin with the heel of his right palm sending him backwards and landing on the floor, stunned. Mike not giving him a chance to think, quickly kicked with his right foot and caught the stunned man in the face knocking him out.

DJ, caught up in the action, punched the man near him in the face with his fist, sending him over another table. Mike, with his right leg, back kicked the third man in the stomach ending any threat to their departure.

The owner was yelling in Chinese and had picked himself up from the floor. Mike grabbed him by the shirt collar and said.

"I don't like anyone threatening me and trying to keep me where I don't want to be. Let this be a lesson to you." He pushed the owner away and turned in the direction of the restrooms and yelled.

"Hey Sue, you ready yet?"

"Okay, ok, I'm coming." And Sue walked out of the lady's room. When Mr. Ye saw that, his mouth fell open and he sat down mumbling to himself in Chinese.

The other patrons in the restaurant took advantage of the situation and left without paying their bills. Out on the sidewalk, in front of everyone, Mike said to Sue. "Take us home." And in front of everyone from the restaurant, they vanished.

The three time travelers were back in Mike's house so fast, DJ almost fell over.

"That was fast." He said

"Yeah, I still haven't gotten used to it, Sue does things so fast sometimes, it scares me."

DJ looked at his watch and said. "Mike I have to get going, I'm on the night shift this week."

Mike took DJ by the shoulders.

"DJ my old friend, you have nothing to worry about. You call up your boss and tell him you quite."

"I can't do that I need the money."

"DJ. DJ you haven't been listening to what I've been telling you, you're my partner. And from now on you won't have to work for your money. We're going on one big adventure, money is no object."

"Oh yeah, I suppose you're going to break out a couple of barrels of greenbacks you've been hiding and let me dig in. Seriously Mike, I've got to get back." Mike looked at his friend.

"Oh yee of little faith, don't you realize what we've got here?" Mike said pointing at Sue.

"Go ahead DJ, ask Sue if there's anything she can't do, go on ask her."

"Mike after what I've seen today, I don't think there's anything she can't do, but I don't think she can pull money out of thin air."

"No that's not what her mission is, but you gave me an idea back there at the restaurant.

"Yeah, what was it?"

"Remember you said something about going back and getting money that was no longer in existence?" "Yeah, I remember that."

"Well, you go home and gather up all your belongings, bring them out here and move in with me, and we'll plan our first trip."

"Okay, now you're talking." The idea was right up his alley.

"But it's going to take me a couple of days to get my things together and come back here."

"No it won't, Sue, I would like you to go with DJ to his place and help him bring back anything he wants. DJ, you can use the upstairs bedroom."

"What ever you say Michael." And before the words stopped echoing in his head they were gone.

Mike went into the bedroom and removed the box of treasure from the closet and brought it into the living room and put it on the table. He took the pieces out one at a time and examined them each for about a minute or so. He was going over in his mind everything that happened so far. His first trip into the valley. The disastrous second trip into Tut's chambers. He had always wanted to go back and visit ancient Egypt, even before Sue came on the scene. He thought to himself.

"I've got to go back there again, maybe this time we'll just take a boat and sail down the Nile." "We'll take a camcorder along for some pictures." Just then a thought hit him, and DJ came walking down the stairs. "Your right about one thing Mike, Sue sure is fast." Mike turned around.

"Good, I'm glad your back, Sue, I have an idea."

"Yes Michael I know, everything is as you want, there is a forty foot yacht waiting for us on the Nile." "Sue, you never stop amazing me, but I wish you wouldn't read my mind like that, I may have some very personal thoughts." "Michael, you know I've been in your mind ever since we united on the hill, we have a permanent link that can only be broken by your death."

"Your right, I forgot." DJ cut in.

"What's this about a yacht on the Nile?"

"While you two were gone, I came up with an idea." DJ pulled a chair out and sat down. He started to look at the treasure. "Great, what's your idea, I hope it's something that will make us some money?" "It will in the long run, but it's just something I have to get out of my blood."

"I'm game, what can I do to help?"

"You've always been good with a camera, I'd like you to just take pictures, stills and with a camcorder." "Hell, that's one of my favorite hobbies. From what Sue just said, I assume we're going to ancient Egypt." "Right, first we'll go back and take lot's of pictures, then we bring them back, show them to another archeologist, sort of like bate. And then, after their hooked, we start making money."

DJ was fingering a necklace and said. "If I remember correctly, you charged Jim and co. a grand an hour, right?" "Yeah, why?"

"A grand an hour is not really going to make us rich overnight." Mike looked at his friend and said.

"Look at it this was DJ, we get the right people hooked on this and we're talking trips of two maybe even three days at a clip. Hell, maybe even a week, now that's big money." DJ put down the necklace and looking at Mike said. "Yeah, but who's going to pay for such a long trip, unless I miss my guess, most Museums don't have unlimited funds available to them."

"Yeah, but some museums have rich patrons who will donate money at the drop of a hat, we just have to find the right one. Besides, an opportunity like this will only come around once in a life time."

"Great, how do we do that?" DJ asked. Mike looked at Sue.

"Sue, you keep telling me there's nothing you can't do." "Yes Michael?"

"Good, which museum do we hit first?"

"I found a small museum in a small town outside Reno Nevada."

"Reno, well at least if we come up short on that one, we can do a little gambling." DJ said

"Okay, now that that's settled, why don't we just retire for the night, you know, sit around and watch a little boob toob and suck down some brew."

"Now your talken, where's the brew?" Mike stood up an stretched.

"As long as the boat awaits, why don't we retire to ancient Egypt and get things started?"

"You mean, go there tonight? What about supplies, weapons, cameras, food?"

"Hell when we get there we can make a list while we watch the TV. Sue can get what we want in a heart beat, right Sue?" "That's right Michael." Mike looked at his friend.

"You ain't chickening out on me are you?" DJ stopped playing with the jewelry. "Well it is kinda sudden." "So, the sooner the better, are you ready?" DJ looked at his two companions and said.

"Why the hell not, let's go." Mike was about to tell Sue to do her thing, when he remembered something. "One more thing before we go, Sue did you take all necessary precautions?"

"Yes Michael, everything is taken care of." Mike walked over to Sue and put his hands on her shoulders. "I hope you had the fore thought to make the boat invisible?"

"Yes Michael, its invisible." "Good, then if there's nothing else, let's go."

And before Mike had finished saying, "go," they were there.

"Holy shit Mike, is she always this fast?"

"Yeah, scary, isn't it?"

They looked around at the yacht that Sue had drummed up for their little adventure.

"Man this is some piece of work." DJ said sitting down in one of the four leather recliners in what was the living room. "I could get used to something like this, no sweat."

Mike was walking around touching everything, the chairs, the drapes on the windows; he bent down and felt the plush carpet. "Where did you ever get this from?" He asked Sue.

"I searched your memories and found this, you saw this when you were a little kid at a boat show."

Mike thought for a moment. "If you say so, but I really don't remember going inside any of them."

"You didn't, but this is what it was like." DJ picked up the remote control for the 27-inch color TV and pushed the on button. "Hey, Mike, I didn't know they had TV in ancient Egypt?" Mike looked at the picture; it was a Married with Children rerun. "They didn't, it's just Sue."

"Yeah, yeah I know I shouldn't have asked. But the picture is great."

Mike and DJ made a quick check of the yacht; it was everything they could have asked for. It had a big eat in kitchen, just enough room for about six people. When they got to the engine room, DJ asked. "How is this thing powered?" Sue said.

"I equipped it with a battery that I acquired from another civilization from the other side of your galaxy." Mike looked at the thing Sue was pointing at. "A battery?"

"Your world won't have the know how to make one of these for at least a thousand years."

"But why a battery?" DJ asked

"Well for one thing, it's very powerful and very quite, and there's no gas stations anywhere near the Nile." "Hey Mike, Sue got a sense of humor." "Yeah, I've been noticing that, but right now I think we should retire to the living room, pop open a beer and make a list of the things we're going to need."

Back in the living room, they sat down opened some beer, turned on the television and sat back. "Okay, DJ, what do we need?" Mike asked his partner and friend.

"Well if we're going to take pictures, stills and tape, we're going to need top of the line equipment. But I'd rather we had something we can easily carry, as opposed to the big bulky things the TV news stations carry around." Mike thought for a second.

"DJ, I don't know what the fuck your talken about. Sue do you?"

"Yes Michael, I know exactly what DJ needs." And no sooner had she spoken the words, but it appeared on the table in front of them. DJ put down his beer, his eyes widened.

"Holy shit, I never seen anything like this before." He picked up the camcorder Sue had produced and was playing with it. "Its technology from your future." Sue said. DJ was engrossed in the camera. "Well DJ, I see you're happy with your new toy." Mike said downing his beer.

In the course of an hour, they compiled a list of needed supplies, all of which were stored on board as soon as they where asked for.

"I'm happy with the list, how about you DJ?" Mike asked "Yeah, it suits me just fine, I like the M-14's, that's a nice touch, you can never be to safe I always say."

"Yeah, I've always like the M-14, it has a nice feel to it. And besides I fired expert with it in the corps."

They sat back and watched TV, about 10PM, after consuming about a case of beer; the two time travelers fell asleep in their chairs.

"Michael, its eight o'clock in the morning, do you want to start on your journey now?"

Mike rubbed his eye's to get the sleep out of them. DJ heard Sue and woke up also.

"Man that was a good nights rest. I don't know about you, Mike but I'm famished."

"Yeah, I could go for a good breakfast right about now, but first I think I'll go on deck and piss in the Nile." DJ was standing up and stretching, "You took the thought right out of my mind." And the two of them walked up on the deck, Mike went to the rear and DJ went to the starboard side.

"The air smells a little musty, I thought all the pollution didn't start until the industrial revolution?" DJ was standing at the rail when he noticed Sue standing there watching them.

"Uh Mike, I really can't take a piss with Sue standing here watching." Mike turned around and saw Sue looking at them. "Sue can we have a little privacy please."

"Michael, I was programmed to note and examine all aspects of your life for the home planet."

"I thought you told me your home world didn't exist anymore?" "It doesn't, but my programming is still intact. Besides why would you care, I'm really not human."

"Well DJ, she's got a point there." DJ was doing a little jig about this time.

"Oh what the fuck, I gotta go." He unzipped his fly and let loose."

"Here Sue, let the folks at home watch this." And DJ arched his back and aimed for the shore.

"I'm going for distance Mike." Again the two friends laughed.

"Hey Mike, I thought you said this boat was invisible?"

"Yeah, it is, why?"

"Well unless I'm mistaken, there's two people over there in the reeds watching us."

Mike and Sue turned to look where DJ was pointing.

"There, about a 25 yards from the shore."

"I'll be damned, your right. Sue, I thought we were invisible?"

"We are Michael." Mike grabbed a pair of binoculars that were laying on the deck chair and peered at the faces in the reeds. "I see a man and a women, and I think there are a couple of kids also." "Let me see Mike." DJ took the binoculars from Mike and looked.

"So, Sue how do you account for that?"

"Michael, I can tell you what's going on in the area from my position above."

"Okay, what's going on?" Mike and DJ zipped up their pants and turned to Sue.

"These people come from an Egyptian fort about two miles from here. The fort is under attack by a band of Nubian warriors. These people managed to escape from the raiders because they were on the outside of the fort picking vegetables when they heard the attack begin. I see about seven Nubian warriors searching for the family."

"But how can they see us?" Mike asked.

"From what I can gather from the man's mind, he is a fisherman by trade, and yesterday while out on the Nile, his small skiff came across the depression in the water left by this boat. He left the area very quickly and returned to his wife. He related everything to her. He had to tell some one, because he is convinced that only a god could have a boat that can't be seen. He couldn't tell anyone else because of Pharaohs edict that all Egypt should worship only one god, the sun."

"Okay, you brought us back to the time of the reign of Ackenaten"

"Yes Michael, I thought you'd like to start you journey at this point in time."

"Yes, very good Sue, but why is this family here now?" "Well the man figures that if there is a god on the Nile, maybe he will save this man and his family from the Nubians. You see Michael, if the Nubians catch the family, they will rape and torture the girls and women in front of the man before they torture the man in front of his family. Then they will kill them." Mike looked at the man and then said to Sue. "How many Nubians did you say were looking for the family and how far away are they?" "There are seven warriors searching and they are right over there." Sue said pointing to the approaching warriors." DJ turned the binoculars on the warriors. "Ugly mothers, what do you say Mike, we have no prime directive to stick to." "Your right DJ, get us a couple of M-14's and some ammo." "Now you're talking my language." And DJ ran down the steps to get the weapons.

When he returned with the rifles, Mike said

"You're just in time DJ, the warriors spotted the family. You take the second one I got dibs on the first, then the rest, okay?" "Got you Mike."

The family saw the warriors coming and fell down on their faces praying to the god in the boat to save them. The girls were screaming from terror, which only spurred on the warriors. Mike and DJ took careful aim. Mike said

"At the count of three. One, two, three." The first two shots brought down the two leading Nubians, and the report from the rifles brought the others to an abrupt halt. Seeing their comrade's heads explode at the same time they heard the load noise. The remaining warriors turned to flee from they didn't know what, but didn't want to hang around to find out. Mike and DJ kept firing until all the warriors had been killed.

Upon hearing the noise coming from the direction of the boat in the water, and seeing the Nubian warriors die. The man was convinced his prayers were answered. He stood up to see if all the warriors were gone then turned towards the boat and again bowed low.

"Sue, I want you to speak to the man using a deep male voice, tell him you are the god Amon Ra. Tell him that he and his family are safe, tell him you are aware of what's happening at the fort. And that you are going to come to the aid of the others in the fort." Sue did as Mike asked the man and his family, hearing the voice of the king of the god's looked at each other and if it were possible they got closer to the ground. The man began to tremble, he suspected there was a god here, but never had he imagined it would be the king of the gods. Sue continued.

"Come my true and faithful servant, bring your family closer." Sue translated what she had said to the man for Mike and DJ. "I see a problem arising here. If we're going to interact with these people, we're going to have to understand them and them us."

"Yeah, you're right, so, what do we do?"

"Sue, can you whip up a spell or whatever you call it?"

"I already did Michael, you can now understand them and they you."

DJ looked at Mike. "She don't fuck around does she?"

"No, you'll get used to her speed." As they were talking the man and his family started to come closer to the boat.

"Sue, I'm a buff on ancient Egypt, and I don't remember Nubia invading Egypt during Akenatens reign?" While the family started to walk closer to the invisible boat, Sue said.

"Michael, let me give you a brief history of Egypt in this dimension."

"All of Egypt's enemies know pharaoh is weak, he has neglected his army. It is weak and demoralized. They haven't fought a war in about 25yrs. About a year ago, the Hittites sent two boats down along the coast and made contact with the Nubians. The Hittites have developed iron. They made a pact with the Nubians to launch an attack on Egypt from the north and south at the same time. This little raid is to show the Nubians how effective their iron swords are against the bronze of the Egyptians." Mike understood what Sue was saying; Egypt was weak at this time because Acknaten cared more about his sun god, than he did about the welfare of his people or his country.

The family had made their way closer to the boat and were now kneeling and bowing low at the edge of the river. "Sue, tell the family that Ra is sending two of his warriors to destroy the Nubians attacking the fort. Tell them that it is safe for them to start back to their home by the time they get there the fight will be over. Sue spoke to the family and the father led them away. Mike and DJ replenished their supply of ammo. Mike asked.

"How do you think we should do this DJ? Should we fix bayonets and come at them from different sides or what?" "Well as long as we are going to be warriors sent by Ra, why don't we come out of the clouds? You know, like Sue could bring us down slowly and place us in a position were we could see all of the Nubians at once."

"Hey, that's a great idea, Sue, do you get the picture? Can you bring us down from the clouds like we were being sent by a god?"

"Yes Michael, I will place you the highest points on the walls were you can see all of the enemy." Mike looked at DJ. "Are you ready for battle my friend?"

"I'm ready as I'll ever be, with a magazine and twenty rounds, lock and load." The two warriors of Ra gave each other the high hand shake and turned to Sue."

"Okay Sue turn on the recorder, the folks on your planet are in for some action. We're ready, send us."

No sooner had Mike said that than they were descending out of the blue. The battle for the fort was going hot and heavy. The Nubians had caught the Egyptians by surprise. A lot of the families were outside the wall's tending the gardens of vegetables growing to help feed the population of about three hundred people living there. Most of the civilians living there were families of the officials and the soldiers stationed at the fort. The tribute sent from Nubia and all goods traveling on the Nile had to stop at this station and the officials would check it and make an accurate list, which was to be sent along to the city of the Aten.

The few people who couldn't escape the Nubians were killed, the prettiest of the women were being returned to Nubia for the pleasure of the Prince. The attacking force numbered about seventy-five warriors. The Egyptian force numbered around fifty. Most of the fighting was being done from the walls of the fort; archers were firing their arrows at the enemy outside the walls. A small force numbering around twenty-five was just leaving the fort to confront the Nubians. Mike told Sue in his mind to make a loud noise as he and DJ were coming down "You know, for effect."

There was a loud, deep rumbling noise from the sky that caught everyone's attention. All around and inside the fort stopped for a brief moment to look up. They were coming down like birds, surly they were gods.

"Hear me Nubia, the sun you see in the sky will be the last one you ever see, I am Ra, king of the gods of Egypt. You will pay for attacking my people." Sue had added that touch her self, Mike said to her in his mind. "Nice touch Sue, nice touch."

"Okay DJ, pick your target and give um what for."

"All's ready on the firing line, ready, aim, FIRE."

Mike started firing at a group of Nubians amassing to meet the group of Egyptians coming out of the gate. DJ noticed a small group of Nubians leading away several young girls who they captured. He took careful aim and killed three of the five warriors without hitting the girls. The other two kept running. By now Mike and DJ were standing on the wall firing at the fleeing black warriors. Their appearance from out of the clouds and the pronouncement from Sue saying she was Ra, had given the defending Egyptians new life the twenty –five men who had just left the fort, now screaming at the tops of their lungs, were chasing the fleeing enemy and cutting them down like wheat in the field.

The descent of the two strange gods from the sky, coupled with their comrades being killed by loud noises, sent the remaining Nubians on their way back to Nubia. The few that couldn't out run the Egyptians were caught. Mike and DJ were positioned on the walls of the fort were they had the best field of fire. The Nubian warriors caught and being returned to the fort were being clubbed and kicked by the Egyptians. The girls being taken back to Nubia were returned. Mike and DJ climbed down from the walls and walked towards the center of the compound. Everywhere they looked, people were on the ground, heads bowed and arms stretched out bowing to the two gods who had descended from the skies to save them from the Nubians.

As the warriors returned to the fort, they also bowed. Mike and DJ were surprised to see even the Nubian warriors bowing. For everyone here had seen these two descend from the clouds, surly they were gods. "Well DJ, I've got to hand it to you, coming out of the clouds was a nice touch. As far as these people are concerned, we're gods."

"Yeah, it seems that way. But I'm a little weary of being considered a god."

Mike had asked Sue to make communication easier between them and the Egyptians. Mike walked over to one person who looked like he was someone important.

"What is your name?" And he nudged the man with his foot. The man started to shake.

"You, I'm speaking to you, get up man and speak to me, what is your name and who are you?"

Again Mike poked him with his foot only a little harder. The man got up slowly, not wanting to anger this god any further. He stood, head bowed hands raised in front of him at eye level.

"My name is Hopi, I am the captain of the guards."

"I want to speak to your soldiers in the square, assemble them and bring all your officials."

"I hear and obey." And the man turned and calling to several others walked in the direction of soldiers.

Mike and DJ called for all the people to get up and go about their business. They walked over to where the soldiers were assembling. As they approached, all of those waiting for the gods to arrive, fell to the ground bowing.

"Arise my friends, we are not gods, merely soldiers of Ra." Everyone got up and looked at each other. As Mike spoke to the assembled, he pointed up to the ball of light that hovered over the compound. Sue spoke to the warriors.

"Hear these words, these standing before you are my servants and warriors. Treat them as you would treat me were I among you, listen to them and obey." As soon as Sue started to speak, again every one fell to the ground. Was not the king of all the gods speaking to them? Mike told everyone to get up, and pointing up in the air again, everyone saw Sue disappear.

"Who is the officer?" Mike asked. A man stepped forward and bowing his head and putting his hands up spoke. "I am great one." The man looked no older than his late twenties or early thirties

"What is your name?" Mike asked. "I am called Seti great one."

"Seti, do you have a place you can put the prisoners until we bring them to pharaoh?"

"Yes lord, we can put them in with the cattle."

"Then do so." "DJ, this is what I have in mind." Mike related to DJ a plan he had thought up. He wanted to take the dead Nubians and drop them in on the prince that had thought up this raid on Egypt, and to show him what he was up against if he carried out his plans with the Hittites.

"Yeah, I like that Mike."

"Good, would you take about a dozen men and gather up the dead Nubians and put them in a pile outside the walls?" "Sure thing Mike." And DJ turned to the assemble warriors and asked for twelve men to follow him. After all the warriors were piled up outside the walls and the captured men were tied up and in with the cattle, Mike turned to the captain and said. "Captain, you and your men follow us." Mike and DJ walked over to a large clearing in the middle of the fort, there Mike and DJ turned to face the Egyptian warriors.

The captain and his men stood in a circle around the two gods, they started to bow again, but Mike stopped them. "No, no, stand up we are not gods, only warriors and servants to Ra, like you are to Pharaoh. Ra has sent us down here not just to help you fight the Nubians." Mike in his mind had asked Sue to conjure up swords that would cut through the Hittites iron like a hot knife through butter. At a given signal from Mike the swords were to appear in the middle of the circle where he and DJ were standing. Mike continued to talk to the assembled warriors, he told them all that was happening between the two enemies of Egypt, to its north and south. He reinforced what they already suspected about Pharaoh.

"I see some of you have already taken the swords the Nubians were carrying. You have discovered that their swords are made of a stronger metal than what you have." "Ra knows this and has made swords that are much stronger than the iron of the Hittites." And Mike pointed to a spot between himself and DJ. A flash of bright light appeared and everyone covered their eyes and stepped back. There on the ground appeared a pile of bright shiny swords. There were mutterings and mumbling from the assembled warriors, never had they seen such miracles.

Mike pointed to one of the men standing in the front; the man had one of the Hittite swords.

"Come here my friend." He said pointing at the man. The warrior hesitated, then came forward and fell on his knees in front of Mike.

"Arise my friend and strike at the sword he holds." Mike pointed to DJ who had one of the bronze swords the Egyptians carried. "Go on strike the sword." The man got up; the mere thought of striking at any god meant certain death. He tried to think what he had done to deserve death, but couldn't. He started to shake, and again fell to his knees and then prostrated himself before this god. Mike didn't know what was happening and looked puzzled. Then Sue spoke to him the old way. "Michael, this man thinks you are going to kill him, striking at a god means certain death. He thinks he has offended you in some way." Mike smiled and reached down and put his hand on the mans shoulder. "Stand up my friend, you did nothing to offend us, I am just going to demonstrate something." At these words, the man got up. Surly this is a god; he must have read his thoughts.

"Hold your sword out DJ, here, strike at the sword." The man got his shaking under control and struck at DJ's sword. The bronze weapon broke in half. Again mumbling from the warriors.

"Now, take one of these swords." And Mike handed the man one of the swords Sue had produced. DJ had taken the iron sword from the man and held it out.

"Strike the iron of the Hittites." The man was examining the new shiny sword given him by this god. It was lighter than any sword he had ever seen or held, he looked at Mike and Mike nodded his head giving the man the go ahead. The warrior struck at the sword held by DJ and cut it in half. Again mumbling from the warriors.

Mike walked over to the warrior and said to him. "The sword is yours to keep." And looking around at the other warriors, he said. "And there is one for each one of you, come forward and we will give you each one. After you have gotten used to them, I will tell you how we are going to use them in the service of Egypt." The warriors came closer and DJ and Mike handed out the swords to the men. As each received his new weapon, they smiled and were talking and laughing with each other. They paired off and were practicing with their new weapons.

Mike pulled the captain aside and he and DJ explained to him exactly what they were going to do. Mike wanted to go down to Nubia and bring the dead warriors with them. He told the captain to pick out two of his men to accompany them. The captain called out to two of his men to come over to him. The two he chose were the most experienced men he had, they were both in their thirties and been soldiers the longest of all his men. The men were briefed on what was going to happen and were anxious to accompany the two warriors of Ra into Nubia.

Sue was instructed to make the trip to Nubia as fast and as painless for the Egyptians as possible. The idea of flying through the air was as foreign to them as ice cream. Since Mike and DJ had descended into the compound from out of the sky, the three Egyptians were told that they would be coming down out of the sky. And that they were not to be afraid because Ra was handling everything.

The prince and his generals and Hittite guests were gathered in the courtyard of the prince's palace. A banquette was in progress. All were celebrating the coming war and expected victory over the hated Egyptians. For hundreds of years Nubia and the Hittites had worn the yoke of servitude to Pharaoh. They were tired of sending tribute to Pharaoh's court. It was time to cut off the chains of slavery. The raid was put together to show the Nubians just how effective the iron of the Hittites was against the bronze swords of the Egyptians.

Everyone was in a relaxed and festive mood. The food was plentiful and the beer and wine came from bottomless jars. The sun was high over the distant mountains and the day was hot. DJ had suggested that Sue should approach the Nubians from out of the sun like the fighter planes of WWII.

One of the Hittite soldiers already to drunk to stand was lying with his head in the lap of pretty young maiden. She was feeding him small pieces of fruit. Trying hard to keep awake, he was putting a lot of work into keeping his eyes opened. He was looking into the eyes of the girl feeding him when something just to the left of the girl's face caught his attention. He noticed a bright light sitting there and assumed it was the sun. When he saw movement from the light he jumped up and pointed to the light, calling everyone's attention to what he had seen.

Suddenly there was a loud pop, and then a booming male voice was heard that shook the very walls.

"Hear Nubia and obey, I am Amon Ra, king of the gods of Egypt. You have attacked my people, raping an pillaging. You have broken the treaty that was made between your countries and Egypt. Here is the fruit of your folly." And Sue dropped the bodies of thirty-five dead Nubian warriors from a thousand feet. When they hit the ground many broke apart. Splattering the assembled guests with blood and body parts. Those who had not fainted from fear at the sound of the voice from the sky were on their faces bowing or were crying at the prospect of the end of their lives.

When the bodies fell, everyone was convinced it was the end. "Arise and see the might of the gods of Egypt." No one moved. With a louder voice Sue again spoke. "I said arise or I will destroy you were you lay." All in the courtyard jumped to their feet, a gasp echoed through the crowd and all eyes were looking at the five descending figures.

Sue had dressed the five warriors of Ra in the finest Egyptian fashion. Even pharaoh didn't have such as they wore. As they got closer to the ground, those assembled in the courtyard scattered in all directions. Upon reaching the ground, the three Egyptians took up a defensive posture, as if they were going to be attacked. The five gods that had descended from the sky had a glow about them. Another touch thought up by Sue.

Mike looked over at the captain and gave the prearranged signal. Mike and DJ started to walk over to the prince and Hittite generals. The captain and his two men walked over to a group of Hittites. "Draw your sword Hittite." the captain said to the nearest man. Each of the Egyptians stood before a Hittite. The Hittites looked at each other and thinking to themselves it would be certain death and plane stupidity to draw a sword on a god.

"I said draw your sword and strike at us." The captain said a little louder. Now the Hittites started to draw their swords. Again they looked at each other and thinking that as long as they were going to die, they may as well go out fighting. So as if by pre arrangement, they drew out their swords and with a war cry, aaaah, they struck at the gods standing before them. The Egyptians raised their swords and blocked the downward slash of the Hittites. Upon making contact with the swords held by the gods, the Hittite iron swords shattered. Shocked exclamations arose from the gathered warriors. Now the three Egyptians walked over to one of the stone columns and struck at it with the new metal. The swords sliced into it like it was hanging meat. And again the assembled warriors marveled at what they were seeing. Mike and DJ were near the Nubian prince and his Hittite guests. "You have angered the gods and Ra has sent us to warn you." The prince and the Hittites fell to their knees, heads bowed.

Mike told the captain to take his men and with their swords sever the heads of three dead Nubians. They were told to impale the heads on spears and to give them to three Hittites and instruct them to hold the spears high. Then Mike turned to the prince.

"Your treachery has angered the gods, and we were sent to warn you. The gods are merciful and forgiving." Turning to the Hittites Mike said.

"Your iron is like clay to the metal of the gods." Then turning back to the assembled warriors Mike said. "See what wonder weapons the gods have created to defend the borders of Egypt." And with that DJ lifted the M-14 he was carrying and held it up for all to see. He faced the three Hittites holding the impaled heads and took careful aim. He fired three shots in rapid succession hitting all three heads before the startled warriors could drop the spears.

Never had such noise been heard, the crowd in the courtyard again dropped to their knees this time holding their ears. There was much crying and wailing for all thought the end had come.

"See the power of the gods of Egypt. Know this Nubia, if you cross the border again you will not get a warning like this." Mike was pointing to the Hittites as well as the Nubians when he spoke.

"You will be destroyed and your countries turned into desert. Do you understand?" He waited for some response from the trembling enemies of Egypt.

"Well do you?" Mike raised his voice. The prince looked up from his kneeling position and spoke.

"We hear the words of Amon Ra and will obey."

"Good. You, Hittite, you and your men return to your ships now." The trembling Hittites fell over each other trying to obey this god standing before them. Mike closed his eyes and bowed his head. He lifted his arms in the manner of the Egyptians. He was speaking to Sue, but all thought he was communing with Amon Ra.

"Sue I want to send the Hittites back to their country so they can't make plans again after we leave."

"Yes Michael, I understand. But there is something you should know."

"What?" "Michael the Hittites are on the move, three days ago they left their capital and are heading for Egypt." "Shit, did you hear that DJ?"

"Yeah, I heard. Listen Mike, I have an idea."

"Good, what is it, I'm open for suggestions."

"Okay, we want to delay the Hittite force for awhile, until we can get pharaoh off his ass to act, right?" "Yeah, what's your idea?"

"Put the Hittites we have here in the ships and let Sue take them and drop them down in front of the advancing Hittite army. That should make them stop and think."

"DJ, you never stop amazing me. I like your idea, what do you think Sue?"

"It will be done as you want Michael." Mike thought for a moment.

"No input, no ifs ands or buts?" "None Michael, it will be done as you want."

"You sure you don't have a, look out Michael if you do this thing something bad will happen, up your sleeve?" "No Michael, I am here to do as you want."

"Yeah, yeah I know. Okay as soon as they're all assembled and ready, make it so."

As the five warriors of Ra walked out of the courtyard towards the waiting Hittites, DJ spoke.

"I don't know about you Mike, but I'm so thirsty I could drink Nile water."

"Come to think of it, I could use a drink also." Mike turned to the three Egyptian.

"Captain, are you and your men thirsty?"

"Yes great one."

"Why didn't you say so?"

"We know we will drink sooner of later. We wait for Ra to say rest."

"Okay, you and your men return to the banquet and help your selves to whatever you want. Then meet us over there." Mike said pointing to the waiting Hittites." The three Egyptians bowed and turned back to the courtyard.

When the Egyptians entered the courtyard, everyone scattered. The Nubians were examining the bodies dropped from the sky. The Egyptians walked over to where the food was being prepared and helped themselves to some fruit and fish, each one grabbed a small clay jar of wine. "I would like to have my way with that one." One of the men said pointing to one of the serving girls.

She was not Nubian; she was one of thirty girls the Hittites brought with them as gifts for the prince. She and her friends were taken prisoner when the Hittites raided a small fortified town. The captain looked at the girl and said.

"She is fair of face and has a pleasing figure, but I don't think we have time for that. Maybe if you ask the god, he will let you take her with you." The man grabbed the girl by the arm and ran back to Mike. When he got to Mike he dropped down on his knee's pulling the girl with him. "May I speak great one?"

"Yes, of course."

"Great one you said we could take what we wanted."

"Yes and I see you have good taste in women, do you want her?"

"Yes great one, I would take her as a slave."

"Well I don't condone slavery, but you may take her back with you if she wishes to go."

Mike turned to the girl and asked,

"What is your name girl?" Sue spoke to Mike in the old way

"Michael, she is Israeli, she is one of thirty girls brought here by the Hittites as gifts."

"Ask her again, she will understand you this time." Mike grabbed the girl by the arm and helped her to stand. "What is your name girl?" he asked again. The girl's eyes opened wide and she fell at Mike's feet upon hearing her own language and cried. She lifted her head, tears streaming down her face and said.

"Please take me and the others with you, please?" she was holding on to Mikes legs with an iron grip. "What is your name girl?"

"My name is Rachel, we were taken prisoner by the Hittites and taken back to their city, then they brought us here and gave us to them." She said pointing to the Nubians. She continued.

"And they made us salves, and made us strip and walk around for days naked and then and then." Mike put out his hand on patted her on the cheek.

"Wait, wait slow down girl, where are the others you speak of?"

"I don't know, they are here someplace, please take us with you Please."

"Yes we will help you, DJ, Do you want to handle this?" DJ looked at the girl and felt pity for her, she was young, probably no older than 16.

"Yeah Mike, I'll get the rest of them. I'll take the captain and the other man and we'll meet you at the pier shortly."

"Okay, I'll take the other one and we'll be with the Hittites waiting. Sue will help you if you need some special effects." Mike and the one man turned and walked towards the boats. DJ and the man and girl returned to the compound where the captain was waiting.

DJ walked over to where the prince and his generals were standing.

"You, Nubian." DJ said pointing to the prince.

"I have come for the rest of the girls she came with." DJ said pointing to Rachel.

When the five visitors from the sky had left the compound, the prince called his chief priest over. The prince wanted to know how could the Egyptian gods have any power here in Nubia. But the priest was powerless to help, he had seen what this Egyptian god could do, he knew in his heart the gods he prayed to were false. This Egyptian god, really was a god. He was about to tell his prince just that when DJ returned.

"I am waiting." DJ turned to the captain and said.

"Captain raise you sword over your head." The captain didn't hesitate; he was getting used to all kinds of miracles. DJ was thinking about a bolt of lightening hitting the sword with out hurting the captain. And Sue was reading his mind. Out of the clear blue sky came a bolt of lightening and struck the raised sword. The captain stood his ground, not even blinking.

"The next one will strike you if you do not turn over the girls."

When the lightening struck the priest ran away. Surly only a god could with stand the power of lightening. The assembled nobility of Nubia jumped about a foot off the ground and the prince almost wet himself. Being struck by lightening was not the way he wanted to go.

The prince turned to the remainder of his guards, those who had not run away and said.

"Go bring the slave girls, quickly, lest you displease this god." And off the guards ran, thankful to be out away from that place.

With all the Hittites on their ships, Mike left the lone Egyptian to watch the ships. Sue would keep an eye on them also. Mike returned to the courtyard and stood beside DJ.

"How's it going?"

"So far, so good. The prince here just sent his guards to fetch the other girls."

The guards and the rest of the Israeli girls were returning. They had been gathered up so quickly and roughly, that they thought they were going to die. Several of them were crying. When they arrived in the courtyard, Rachel spoke to them in their native tongue.

"We're going home, we're going home, the Egyptians are taking us home." Now the tears of Fear and sorrow turned to tears of joy. The girls danced around and were hugging each other. All had giving up hope of ever seeing their homes again. The girls that were pregnant continued to cry only louder and started to walk away. Rachel stopped the nearest girl and asked. "Where are you going?"

"We can't go home, ever, we are with child and would never be excepted back. The girl was visibly heart broken and inconsolable. Rachel turned to Mike and said.

"Please, do something, are you not gods?"

She was raised believing there was only one god the God of Israel, Jehovah. But she had seen this god at work and was totally confused. And in an effort to bring home all her friends she turned to this Egyptian.

DJ turned to Mike and said. "Well pal, what now?" Sue spoke to both of them at the same time. "Michael, I can reverse their pregnancies if you wish."

"DJ, I don't want to leave any of these girls here in Nubia, it just wouldn't be right. Okay Sue, tell me what to do." Mike thought in his mind.

"Tell the girls to come forward." Mike turned to Rachel and said.

"Tell your friends who are with child to come forward, we will help them."

Rachel looked from DJ to Mike then called to her friends.

"Wait, come back, this god will help you, please come back." When the girls heard that there was help, they started to walk back. Sue spoke to Mike again and instructed him as what to do with the girls. Mike said to Rachel.

"Rachel, have the girls line up here." There were eight girls in various stages of pregnancy; two were in their seventh month. Mike pointed his sword at the girls lined up next each other holding hands. They were trembling, not knowing what was going to happen.

Mike looked over at the prince and said. "See Nubian, because you saw fit to attack Egypt, your seed is no more. Mike wasn't sure what was going to happen himself. All eyes were on the eight maidens. Suddenly the light that was over the courtyard got very bright, all those gathered below started to shake all over again at the power of this god.

A bright light came from Mike's sword and slowly made its way over to the girls. It surrounded all eight girls then slowly disappeared. The stomachs of the girls slowly returned to normal size and the girls experienced a fresh flow of blood, they were getting their periods again. They looked at each other and started to cry and were hugging each other in their joy.

Mike again spoke to the prince. "Know this Nubia, the next incursion into Egypt and there will be no more seed in all of Nubia." Mike turned to Rachel and said.

"Tell your friends to follow us."

Mike and DJ led the little procession out of the courtyard towards the Hittite ships moored at the pier. The Egyptians taking up the rear. Mike told all the Hittites to board the smaller of the two ships. The girls the Egyptians DJ and Mike would take the other for themselves.

"Okay Sue, take us back to the compound." Mike said looking up at the light still over the Nubian City. "When we get back to Egypt, put this boat down next to ours in the Nile. The other one keep in the air outside of the walls, oh I don't know, maybe 400 feet in the air. Just until we get our thoughts organized."

"What ever you say Michael."

"Wait Sue, we better tell the girls what to expect, I don't want anyone jumping over the side in a panic to stay on land." Mike walked over to Rachel and got her attention.

"Rachel, I want to tell you what's going to happen, we're going to return to Egypt but not by water." Rachel and the others she had been speaking with looked at each other and then back to Mike. "If we went by river, it would take to long. We're going to fly through the air."

Rachel was very quick to pick up on the concept of flying through the air. After all, were not these two gods? She spoke to her companions.

"I am not afraid to fly, after all these two gods wouldn't let us get hurt." She turned to Mike and asked. "Would you?" Mike and DJ smiled and answered

"Of course not, we just wanted to prepare you for something we know you have never done before and we didn't want panic to take over. Okay, we're ready." Mike said looking up at the bright light that was Sue.

When the two ships started to rise out of the water, panic took over on the ship with the Hittites. Men were screaming and running around, some even tried to jump over board just like Mike had suspected. The girls were very nervous; some of them had fainted. Others were just curious and were standing by the rail watching as if this flying were second nature to them. Sue had taken the precaution to put up a barrier around each ship just in case someone got to nervous and tried to jump.

Several of the girls had gotten into a discussion about what god was responsible for what was happening. One of them asked Rachel which god was responsible. After all, Rachel seemed to know these two strange beings. One asked her."

"Rachel, what god is doing this, it must be the God of Israel." Rachel answered.

"I saw what happened in the courtyard, it is the Egyptian god Ra that is doing this."

The girls were very confused; after all they were raised to believe there was only one god. The girl spoke again. "But that is impossible, there is only one God, the God of Israel."

Rachel asked Mike to settle a question.

"Is not the god Ra doing this?" Mike knew this was going to happen and he tried to prepare himself for it. He spoke to all the girls who had gathered around to hear the answer to this question that was on all their minds.

"Let me try to put this in terms you will understand. When you look up into the night sky and see all those stars, you're looking into a vast and endless universe. A universe filled with more suns and planets than there are grains of sand in the desert. And in that vast and endless universe there is only one God. But he is known by many names. So in a way, you are both right." The girls were only a little less confused, but it was enough to know that they were right. So they turned to the more important thing right now, they're flying through the air.

It took Sue only a matter of minutes to get them back to Egypt. She placed the ships as Michael had told her to. The people in the fort didn't know what to make of the Hittite ship suspended in the air out side of the fort. A kind of panic had set in, the gates were locked and the guards were posted on the walls. The little compound had seen both ships flying in the air, but had no idea what was going on. The one stopped outside the walls and the other had continued in the direction of the Nile.

They skimmed low over the compound and headed for the Nile. As the ship slipped into the water next to the yacht, Mike put his hands over his eyes. He wanted to speak to Sue and let everyone think he was communicating with the god Ra. The captain saw what Mike was doing and signaled to his men and the girls to drop to their knees and bow.

"Sue we're going to be here for a couple of days and I want to make the girls comfortable. I was thinking." And Sue cut in.

"And you want to have an oasis out side the fort."

"You've been in my thoughts again."

"I'm part of you remember Michael."

"Yeah yeah I know but I'd like to make the arrangements myself." DJ was hearing all of this and he added. "Hey Mike, how about something like they had in the picture the Ten Commandments? You remember like the pharaohs daughter had."

"Yeah, that would be nice, but I want a larger one so all the people in the compound can enjoy it also. What do you say Sue, can you whip up something like that? But before you do, I'd like a lot of trees and running water." DJ added.

"Hey Mike, how about we show these rubes how Americans through a party, you know like a huge barbecue an lots of beer and wine."

"You know DJ, I'm very happy you agreed to come along, I like the idea, make it so Sue." "As you wish Michael, it's already there."

The guards on the wall expecting some kind of attack from the Hittites were startled when they saw the huge white cloud move in from the Nile. Never before had they seen such as this. Ever since the two gods came out of the sky, strange things have happened. And now this cloud. The guards were pointing at the cloud and talking among themselves, orders were given to close the gate. The people in the compound were starting to panic again. The strange cloud approached the fort and stopped once it had reached and covered the north and west sides. All the guards were up on the walls not knowing what to expect. As the cloud slowly ascended to the sky, a great oasis was exposed, never before had anyone seen such a large oasis. There was running water and grass and trees that no one had ever seen before.

As the guards were marveling over what they were looking at, a voice was heard.

"Open the gate, we are back." It was the captain leading the girls. Michael and DJ were in the rear with Rachel. As they approached the fort and saw what Sue had done, Mike said.

"DJ, I want you to pinch me, I don't believe what I see. Can you believe what's happening here?" "Mike if I didn't see it with my own eyes I wouldn't believe it, I think I'm dreaming because I'm having too much fun."

"I know what you mean, captain, tell the rest of the people in the fort to come out and enjoy them selves." The captain raised his hands and bowed his head to Mike. He turned and shouted to the men on the walls.

"Open the gates and tell the people to come out we are going to celebrate."

When the gates were opened at first those inside hesitated, a guard came out and was greeted by one of the men that had accompanied Mike and DJ to Nubia. Upon realizing it was his friend and everything was all right, he turned and waved to everyone else that it was okay to come out. The people came out slowly at first. But when they saw what was waiting for them, the fort emptied out very quickly.

Mike found a rock and climbed up on it. He raised his hands for everyone to be silent. When the crowd quieted down he spoke.

"My friends, the god Ra has provided this oasis for you because you and the rest of Egypt that suffered under pharaoh long enough. The gods are angry and things in the black land are going to change and become like they were before. As I am speaking to you there is a large Hittite army heading towards the cities in the delta. I am going to send that ship you see up there and place it front of their advancing army and then they will see the power of the gods of Egypt. A long and loud cheer arose from the assembled people. And with that said the Hittite boat slowly moved off the direction of the delta. Mike continued.

"We are going to celebrate the return of the old gods, there's food and drink enough for everyone. Come and enjoy your selves."

The oasis was endless; Sue had opened a portal to a dimension not yet occupied by man. She had taken precaution to eliminate anything, animal or insect that could hurt anyone. It was truly an Eden. There were one hundred barbecue grills, one hundred large kegs of beer and one hundred barrels of wine. As the people settled into eating and drinking, Mike and DJ stood there watching everyone. The priest and local lord in charge of this fort approached them. They bowed and waited for Mike or DJ to say something.

DJ poked Mike in the side. Mike looked over at the small group waiting to be recognized.

"Speak priest, what is it you want?"

"Forgive us great one, but we would like to thank the god's for what they have given us."

Mike looked at the two men kneeling before him and thought to himself. "These people really believed in gods, oh well I might as well play along, I've gone this far."

"Stand up my friends, the gods know how grateful you are, the gods know everything."

The two men stood up but still looked a little nervous. DJ picked up on this and asked.

"What still bothers you that you look like you were going to be run through by an enemy?"

The lord of this fort at the end of civilization, as he always referred to it, spoke.

"It is only that when pharaoh hears of this paradise supplied by the gods, he will send his army to come and destroy us, he will not listen to reason." DJ looked at the shivering man and said.

"Do not fear pharaoh or his god, we will take care of pharaoh, and make him see reason."

Mike added. "In a day or two we will depart for pharaoh's court and he will see the error of his ways." The lord of the fort, one Hopi and the priest were very much relieved at this and backed away from the two gods bowing. Mike said to them.

"Go, enjoy your selves, eat and drink."

"Mike, I don't know about you, but I'm getting hungry and horny at the same time."

"Hell DJ, I'm a step ahead of you, I've even got the girl picked out I'm going to spend the night with." They looked and each other and laughed.

"We'll meet back here in around 24 hours, okay?" Mike asked

"Sounds fair to me Mike, see ya." And DJ walked over to the table piled high with fried chicken.

Meanwhile, back in the compound where the captured Nubian warriors were tied up.

It was just a little piece of iron; he found it on the floor of the forge where his father worked. He picked it up and felt the sharpness. Never had he seen the likes of this. It was strong and very sharp. Stronger and sharper than any piece of metal he had ever seen.

"They will not miss such a small piece of their iron." He thought to himself. He put into the little pouch he had around his neck and walked away. He was right it was not missed.

He showed it to his friends and soon discovered that he was not the only one with a piece of this new metal. Some of them had also found their own. And now he was tied up and sitting among cattle with these same friends. How humiliating. Most of his friends who were also tied up with him had given up hope of ever returning home again. He also had almost given up, but then he remembered the piece of metal in the pouch that he carried with him. Now he was thinking of how to get to it. He kicked the man in front of him. "Ouch, why do you kick me, I am in enough pain from these ropes."

"Do you want to get out of here?" the first warrior asked. The man who was kicked responded. "You must be mad, there is no way out of here." The first man spoke again through clinched teeth. "You are scared, do you see any Egyptians around?" now several of the other men were listening to this conversation.

"What do you suppose to do." Asked another of the men. "Ask the Egyptians to let you go?"

There was laughter from some of the others nearby.

"No fool, think, when did you last see a guard or anyone for that matter?"

They all looked around at each other.

"It was awhile ago." Someone said. "When everyone was running around and shouting something about a cloud, then they all ran out the gate."

"What do you have in mind?" Asked someone else.

The first warrior spoke again. "Listen to me, someone has to reach under my loin cloth and get my pouch out."

"Are you sure you want your pouch or are you trying to get someone to give you some quick sex before you die?" another said, and again laughter.

"Look, I have a piece of the Hittite iron in there and it is sharp. Now who will get it?"

The warrior who was kicked maneuvered himself closer to the one who had kicked him and with much difficulty reached back and found the pouch.

"Now what?" He asked.

"Hold on to it, I will turn around and between us we can open it up."

After several minutes of difficult maneuvering, the two warriors were sitting with their backs to each other.

"Hurry before they return." Another said.

"There I have it, now hold still and I will cut your ropes." The second warrior now free turned around and cut the ropes of the first man. In a matter of minutes all the warriors were free.

"Come, let us escape this place and go home." One of the other men said.

"No wait, first we must find weapons." The first man said.

"I saw the guards go into that building over there." Said another pointing to the guard shack.

All of the warriors followed the first man into the building, soon they all had their swords and some bows and arrows.

"Now let us escape this place before their god sees us." Someone said and the others mumbled their agreement. The first man spoke.

"You can go if you choose, but I am going to kill someone before I go, if I must die, I'll take at least one of them with me." Now the second warrior spoke.

"You are mad, you saw what their metal can do, it is certain death to attack them."

"Go on, go home and tell the others you saw a warrior do his duty."

"We will tell them we saw a mad man attack a god."

Now another spoke. "Wait, we don't know what happened to the Egyptians, this could be a trick to lure us outside the fort were they are waiting for us." Several of the other men mumbled their agreement. "What shall we do?" Another asked. The warrior that was kicked spoke up.

"I will climb the wall and look for them, I am the smallest and the quickest, keep down until I return." The others agreed and tried to melt into the buildings in the area.

The small warrior climbed up to the roof of the barracks and then to the walkway on the wall.

He was fast and quite, soon he was peering over the wall. His eyes widened at what he saw. He couldn't believe what he was looking at. He had never seen an oasis the size of this one, and everyone from the fort was there. He also so saw the girls that the Hittites had presented to his prince. "What were they doing here." He thought to himself. He jumped down; he couldn't wait to tell the others.

"What did you see?" The first warrior asked.

"There is an oasis on the other side of the wall and everyone is there."

"You must be dreaming, there is no oasis around here. When we attacked this morning it was not there, where did it come from, their god?"

"Did you hit your head while you were climbing?" Another asked, and more laughter.

"Listen to me, not only is there an oasis, but I also saw the girls the Hittites brought as a gift to our prince." "Did you also see the prince?" Someone asked. And again more laughter. "We are going, come with us or stay and enjoy the girls at the oasis. The warriors were feeling bolder and braver now that they had their weapons back. They started towards the south wall. The first man spoke to his friends.

"Go if you want, I am going to stay and kill someone." "And I will stay with you." The second man said "Good, we will return home hero's and you will be sorry you didn't stay with us." "You will not live long enough to kill anyone, they will cut you in half with their new metal. We will make a sacrifice to the gods for you as soon as we make camp."

And with those few words spoken all but the first two warriors slipped over the south wall and vanished. The two men waited for the others to slip over the wall. Then armed with their swords and a quiver of arrows and a bow apiece, they climbed on to the wall. The two slowly raised their heads until they could see over the top of the wall,

"See, I told you there was an oasis."

"This is very strange." The first man said. "It was not there this morning when we attacked. It must be a gift from their god Ra." The other warrior added.

"Yes I think you are right, we must be very careful not to be seen." They lowered their heads and sat with their backs against the wall.

"Do you still want to kill someone?" the second warrior asked

"I told the others that I was going to, so now I must. If I don't I will never live it down, I will be called a coward." "No you are wrong, do you not remember their new metal?

Maybe if we can find one of their swords and bring it back with us they will call us hero's?" the second warrior said. The first man looked at his companion and with a smile on his face he said. "I think you are right, with everyone outside we can search for one of their swords and maybe our metal workers can make this new metal. Come, let's start looking." The two warriors jumped down from the wall and started their search.

Standing by one of the barbecues, DJ was trying to explain to a group of people from the fort about 10 of the girls exactly what a chicken was. Most of the people had taken food and were sitting by the lake or exploring the strange forest.

Mike had his own crowd of people to contend with. Several of the girls along with Rachel had cornered him and where pelting him with questions. They wanted to know which god was responsible for all of this. Mike was caught on the horns of a dilemma, he wanted to get some food and just relax and collect his thoughts. But on the other hand he wanted to explain to these Bronze Age people his thoughts on the concept of god.

Rachel, having spent more time with these two strangers than anyone else, was slowly coming to the conclusion that they were not gods themselves, but merely servants of which ever god was responsible.

She knew a god was behind this, did she not fly through the air on a boat meant for the water? And did she not see the other ship hang suspended in the air and then simply float away to the north by its self? Surly only a god could do that. But the question was which god. All her life she was taught that only the Israelites worshiped the true god. And that every other nation worshiped only stone idols.

If only one God existed, then this God must be the God of her people. But stranger yet was the question, if this was her God, why would he be helping the Egyptians? She and her friends were very very confused. Mike put up his hands for silence, he couldn't get a word in with all the girls talking at once.

"Please, please be quite, I can't answer all your questions at the same time. Everyone take some food and follow me over to the lake, we'll find a nice spot to sit down and eat and then I'll try to answer your questions." That seemed to satisfy everyone, and chattering amongst themselves they helped themselves to food from several of the barbecues, took some drink and slowly walked over to the lake. Mike took advantage of the break in questions and walked over to the captain.

"Captain, I was wondering." The captain taken by surprise almost dropped his food trying to kneel down before Mike. "No captain, please remain standing."

"As you wish great one." Mike still wasn't used to being considered a god. He continued.

"Captain I was wondering do you think the prisoners would like some food?" The captain thought this very strange. "Feed your enemy? Why would you waste good food on someone you were going to kill anyway? And if they had captured the fort, they wouldn't feed any of us." The captain thought to himself.

"I don't know great one, would you like to feed them?"

"Yes captain, take one of your men and some of the women and bring them some food and wine. A great man once said it is pleasing to the gods when they see a man being kind to his enemy." Mike paraphrased what Jesus had said about loving thy enemy.

"Consider it done great one." And the captain went and gathered some of the women and one of his men; they put some of the cooked meat and several bottles of wine in a basket and walked off towards the fort.

Inside the fort the two Nubian warriors were quietly going through the building where the captain had his quarters. "Look, here I found them, there are too many for us to take all but we can at least take one each." The first warrior had stumbled on a number of the swords that were put into a large box by the guards for safekeeping. There was no reason to carry them around when everyone was at the oasis. There were no enemies around that would attempt anything with the god present.

As the captain and the small group of people approached the fort a feeling of danger came over the captain. He slowed his pace and put up his hand for everyone to stop.

"What is it captain?" the soldier asked.

"I don't know I sense danger. You and I will enter, you women stay here until I call you."

With that the captain and the guard slowly entered the fort. They stopped just inside the gate. The cattle pen was to the left as you entered but you had to clear the first building to see it. They got close to the building and peered around the corner. The cattle were there but the Nubians were gone. The captain motioned for the guard to return and bring help; he would stay here until the others arrived.

Inside the building the two Nubians were searching for some food. Everything was ready for them to make their getaway. Finding no food, the decided to leave and get something to eat from the Nile. Packing up their weapons they started to leave the building and head for the south wall.

The captain saw the two men emerge from his quarters and head for the south wall. They were carrying two of the new swords given him by the god; he could not let them get away. He drew his sword that he had taken with him to Nubia; he waited for several seconds to see if there were more of the prisoners around. Seeing none he decided to throw caution to the wind and stop them from escaping by himself. By now the guard was returning with the rest of the guards, Mike and DJ were bringing up the rear.

"What is it Mike?" DJ asked. "I'm not sure, I think the prisoners have escaped. And if they did, there could be trouble." The captain had started to run after the two Nubians. He gave his war cry and the two men nearly jumped out of their skins. The two men turned to meet this screaming Egyptian but they were two late, the sword of the Egyptian came down on the head of the first warrior and cleaved him to the breast. The second man seeing his friend die just fell to his knees and surrendered.

The captain was standing over the second warrior about to strike him when Mike and DJ arrived. "Wait, don't kill him." Mike shouted, and the captain lowered his sword to his side.

"How many of the prisoners are still here?" Mike asked.

The captain motioned to two of his men to go and check on the others.

"I don't think we will find any of the others around here great one." The officer replied.

"They are probably far from here by now." Mike looked at DJ and shrugged his shoulders.

"I guess we'll only have one Nubian to bring to pharaoh instead of fifteen."

"It's going to be a tough sell from what you've been telling me about this guy." DJ was referring to what Mike had been telling him about the present pharaoh.

"When do you want to go to see him about the current mess he put Egypt in?"

"Oh I don't know maybe a day or two, I'd like the people to enjoy themselves for a while. And us too before we start the next leg of this adventure."

With the capture of the last remaining Nubian, Mike had one of the women bring him food and with two of the Egyptians watching while he ate, when he was finished he was to be tied up and placed in one of the buildings used for storage. Then the two guards and the women were to come and relax with the rest of the people. The people of the fort, the Israeli girls, Mike and DJ partied into the night and all the next day.

"Michael, wake up Michael." Mike stirred from the deep sleep he was in. With his eyes still closed he lay there trying to remember where he was. There was someone on his chest, with his hand he felt the head, it was a girl. "Oh my aching head." He thought to himself. "I think I over did it last night." He tried drifting off to sleep again.

"Michael, Michael get up."

"Oh mom, there's no school today let me sleep." All of sudden it dawned on him. "Mom is calling me, which means she's near, if she comes in here and finds this girl in my bed." And with that thought in mind, Mike jumped up throwing the girl off of him, she gave a sudden scream and several people around them woke up.

"What the?" looking around he found himself in Egypt at the oasis. The girl he was sleeping with was one of the Israeli girls named Merriam, he had started talking to her about religion and they just hit it off. One thing led to another and they spent the night together.

"Michael I have news for you." Now it all came back to him.

"Oh my head, Sue do you have any magic potions for a hangover?" no sooner had he asked for one, his head stopped hurting. From the next tree he heard DJ say.

"Thanks Sue I needed that."

"You to hah buddy?" Mike asked looking over at his friend lying on the grass with his arm around Rachel.

"Yeah I guess we did a little more partying then we should have."

The sun was getting warm and the people were stirring.

"Michael the Hittites have made camp by the ship I dropped in front of them."

"They made camp? You mean they didn't hightail it out of there?"

"Some of them ran away in panic when they saw the ship coming at them from the air, but the majority of them stayed. They are talking with the men from the ship."

DJ walked over, having heard in his mind what Sue had said.

"If they aren't scared by the power of a god, Egypt is in deep shit."

"I was just thinking the same thing DJ. I think we better pay pharaoh a visit sooner than I planned to. We're going to have to decide who and what to take with us." Mike waved for the captain to come over. "Hopi my friend, something has come up, we're going to leave today for the city of the Aten. I want you and the other two to accompany us."

"As you wish great one."

Ay, councilor to pharaoh, all-powerful in Egypt except for pharaoh. Tossing crumbs into the pool for the fowl. One of many pools in the city of the Aten. This one in the palace set aside for those waiting for an audience with pharaoh. Walking with Ay, is the general of the host of Egypt, Horemheb. Frustration showing on his face.

"Horemheb my friend, I share your frustration, and that pharaoh is a fool all understand. But I don't think he is fool enough to believe that ships can fly through the air."

"I know the report is hard to swallow, but the men who reported this I would trust with my life. If they say they saw a Hittite ship flying through the air, you can believe it was so."

"If pharaoh himself saw the ship flying, he would not send his army against the Hittites. But you may again tell him of your fears that the Hittites are up to something. And you will be wasting your time, he cares not for Egypt only his false god." Horemheb knew Ay was right, pharaoh was a fool.

"There is also the merchant Amos, recently returned from their city with their sword of this new metal iron. You saw the demonstration; it cuts through our swords as if they were made of clay. He must do something when he sees this." Horemheb swung the sword at a stone bench taking a good-sized chunk out of it.

"Yes he will do something, he will send another letter to them asking them to state their intentions. I believe they have at least a hundred such letters. And they will answer with flowery words and praises to his god. And he will not see through their words and again, he will not act no matter what proof you have." Again I share your frustration, I only hope the gods hear my prayers and answer them quickly."

A door to the audience camber opened and a guard walked out, his eyes met those of Ay and a silent message was passed.

"Come my friend, he will see us now." Ay and Horemheb walked together through the doors into the presence of the living god Akhenaten, pharaoh of Kemit. His wife, Nefretity and four of their daughters were present along with his two sons by lesser wives. Smenkara the oldest and the toddler, Tutankaten. Falling on their faces before the living god they were greeted by pharaoh.

"Welcome my two trusted servants, arise and tell me what urgent matter brings you here today?"

Ay stood up and addressed pharaoh. "Hail to you great pharaoh, may the Aten shower you with health prosperity and life everlasting." Pharaoh turned his attention to Horemheb.

"And what urgent matter brings you here today my general?"

"Hail to you great one, may the Aten never turn his face from you." Horemheb stepped forward and knelt down, drawing the iron sword he presented it to pharaoh hilt first.

"I bring you a Hittite sword made of new metal they have discovered. This metal cuts through our swords as if they were made of clay great one, I fear for Kemit more than ever. I beg you let me take your army and destroy the Hittites before it is to late."

One of the guards standing by pharaoh stepped forward and took the sword from Horemheb, he turned to Akhenaten and kneeling down held the sword out for Pharaoh.

Akhenaten reached out with his hand and his fingers barely touched the sword.

"What is this new metal called?"

"It is called iron great one."

"Iron, and because of this new metal you would have me attack my brother?"

"Yes great one, if we do not strike first I fear they will strike at us first, if we strike first we can destroy their forges."

Pharaoh looked at Horemheb and Ay, smiled and said.

"Before we take such drastic measures, let us write to our brother and ask his intentions, I do not seek to war on my brother and I do not think he wants to war against us." Akhentan looked at Ay. "Is there anything else?" Ay looked at Horemheb.

"There is the matter of the report by four officers who were patrolling south of the city on the other side of the river great one."

"And what did they report my councilor?"

Horemheb swallowed and spoke.

"These officers are my most trusted men royal one."

"Yes, what did they report my general, you hesitate to speak, tell me."

Pharaoh picked up on Horemhebs nervousness.

"It was early in the morning, the Aten was still low in the sky, they were watering their horses at the river, when they heard a noise from above them. When they looked up they saw a Hittite ship flying through the air traveling to the north." Akhenaten smiled and asked.

"They saw a Hittite ship flying through the air?"

"Did it have wings like a bird?" Asked Smenkara. There were chuckles from those around the throne. One of pharaoh's daughters spoke.

"Ships can't fly, your men had to much wine." Again more chuckles.

Akhenaten smiled at his children.

"General we all know ships can't fly, my daughter has spoken my thoughts. You don't believe these tales, do you?"

"Great one, as I have said, I would trust these men with my life, I believe what they said."

"Well then my general, I will include in my letter to my brother a question about his flying ships."

And again there were chuckles from those around the throne.

"If there is nothing else, it is time for mid-day devotions to my father. Ay and Horemheb bowed

And backed away from the throne. Horemheb, burning with anger at being made a fool by the girl, Ankesapaten, he would long remember this day

As they walked away from the hall, Ay spoke. "Did I not tell you how it would go?"

"Yes, you did, but I was hoping this new metal would open his eyes. I fear it is too late for Egypt my friend."

"You are a defeatist Horemhed, the gods will not abandon us as he did them."

"I hope you are right, I feel time is running out on us."

Mike and DJ, the captain and the two guards and the Nubian prisoner were walking to the yacht for the trip to horizon of the Aten, Pharaohs City. Several of the Israeli girls had chosen to stay with the Egyptian men they had met. Rachel and Merriam wanted to stay with DJ and Mike, but were talked into returning to their homes with the other girls. They knew what to expect when they did return home, but they figured they could help rebuild their city.

The boat would remain invisible for the journey up the Nile, Mike wanted to get as many pictures and tapes of their trip as he could. Their original reason for coming back to this time. Before they got sidetracked. They could make the trip to speak to pharaoh in a day and a half. Mike wanted to spend the night about a mile from the city so as to make a grand entrance when the day was young. He knew the sight of the yacht would make great impression on the people of the city.As they neared the yacht DJ asked.

"What about the Hittite ship, we just gonna leave it here?"

"Shit I guess so, I forgot about it. It won't hurt to just leave it here until we can think of what to do with it." "Yeah, maybe later we can return and see what we can find on it to sell as antiques."

"Now that's a good Idea."

As they approached the boat, Mike and DJ knew it was there, but the others couldn't see it. Mike spoke to Sue in his mind. He told her that she should be on board when they came and as long as he and DJ were dressed as Egyptians, she should do likewise. "You know." He said to her "When in Rome do as the Romans do."

As they got closer to the yacht, it suddenly appeared. The four residents of this time and place stopped in their tracks. And seeing Sue standing on the ship, they went down on their knees, heads lowered and arms out in the typical Egyptian manner. They were certain they were looking at Isis, mother of Horus and wife of Osiris.

Mike and DJ didn't realize the others had stopped until Sue brought it to their attention.

"Captain, come arise let us get on the ship." The captain got up but hesitated to approach any closer. "What's the matter my friend?" DJ asked walking over to the four.

The captain answered. "Great one, we are not worthy to sail on the same ship as the great goddess Isis." So that was the reason for them stopping. DJ turned and looked at Mike and Sue as if to say "Now what." Mike communicated with Sue.

"Dressed like that, everyone who sees you will think your Isis, do you want to be a goddess?"

"Michael, remember I have no free will, I do as I am instructed."

"Here we go again, all right do you know anything about the goddess Isis?"

"Yes I am acquainted with the history and all the myths of your world."

"Well then you know more then I do. So for the remainder of this escapade, you're the goddess Isis."

"Try not to be to high and mighty, know what I mean?" Mike walked over to the others and said.

"Come my friends, Ra has sent down Isis to help us show pharaoh the errors of his ways. It is all right, Isis expected you, in fact, she chose you out of all the others to accompany her."

The Egyptians looked at each other, and with wonder in their eyes they continued on the yacht. The Nubian prisoner thought to himself. "Truly it was folly to attack these people, we never stood a chance of winning, I only wish I could return and worn the others. Truly their gods are gods, not like the hollow images we worship."

On board the yacht the prisoner was secured to the port railing. The Egyptians were so overwhelmed by the presence of Isis that they couldn't stop shacking. Never had they dreamed they would be this close to a god or goddess. They were always taught that the gods lived in the next world. And at times they doubted they existed at all. And all of a sudden to be in the presence of Isis. They would have some tales to tell when this was over. No one had told them how to act in the presence of a god, they didn't know how to act or if they should even look at her.

Sue under stood what was going on in their minds and spoke with Mike the old way. Mike said to the three men. "Come my friends, Isis wants to talk with you." They were stunned, never did they expect this, this was too much for their minds to comprehend. But Mike was gentle with them, assuring them everything was all right and they had nothing to fear.

Sue played her part to the hilt; she spoke to them as if she had known them from the beginning of their lives. She read their minds and knew all about them. She reassured them that they had nothing to fear and that she had chosen them to be her guards and protectors while she was on this journey. With this news, that they were chosen by the goddess herself over all other men. They felt invincible; even Pharaoh would be envious.

DJ gave them a tour of the ship; he could see the wonder in their faces. Only gods would have a ship as grand as this one. Surly it was built in the next world. There were no rowers, it moved by itself on the water. The beds were as soft as clouds, the chairs were comfortable and the food was the food of the gods. The beer was clear and free of pieces grain like the beer they were used to.

They took turns standing by Sue, you could see the power her words had given them. No one would get with in arms reach of the goddess. They watched Mike and DJ taking pictures and taping the scenery along the Nile, but they didn't understand what was going on.

Mike broke out the binoculars they had stored below, and with great patience showed the Egyptians how to use them. With the wonders that they have seen so far, there was no doubt in their minds that they were among gods.

The sun was just coming up over the distant mountains in the east. The yacht was visible now, but few people stirred in the Harizon of the Aten to see it yet. Pharaoh and his family were in the building that served as a chapel. On the east wall hung a large gold sun disc with gold rays reaching down to the height of pharaoh. Each ray ending in hand. "This." Says pharaoh "Is how the Aten dispenses his blessing." Achtnaten, Neferatiti, their daughters and pharaohs two sons by lesser wives were all present. Also present were several priests and usual complement of guards.

In the streets the first to appear were the merchants and those workers heading to the piers to unload the boats expected to bring supplies from the rest of Kemet and those boats bringing tribute from other lands. Pharaoh had chosen a spot for his new city where it was difficult to grow many crops. It was hard to keep the city supplied with what it needed from the poor soil. So the other cities had to keep the supplies coming.

Achnaten very rarely traveled outside the city dedicated to his god. As long as continued this policy, the other cities were happy to keep him supplied.

DJ called to Mike. "Hey Mike." And he pointed to the north. DJ had seen the lights hanging from the bow of three ships, heavily laden with supplies. The closest one barley two hundred yards away. Mike looked in the direction DJ was pointing and said to Sue.

"Well I guess its time to make our grand entrance."

The yacht was well supplied with lights all along the edges of the deck, sides and cabin. There was also a ten million candlepower spot light controlled from inside the cabin by means of buttons. Not to mention of course a foghorn. DJ called the Egyptian guard's aside and explained to them what was going to happen and that they were not to be scared by the noise they were going to hear it was only for effect.

About twenty workers had arrived on the dock, some were stretching yawning while others had the remains of bread and beer that they had for breakfast. One of them, and old man, he had been deaf for many years. But all the other workers new him and helped him all they could. Mike waited until the approaching ships got a little closer and then he said.

"Okay, countdown, three two one contact." Mike flipped a switch and the yacht lit up like a Christmas tree. He pointed the spotlight at the pier and pressed the button for the foghorn.

Terror reigned supreme. Workers ran in all direction, some fainted others ran leaving trails of body fluids behind. The approaching ships pulled down their masts and stopped their forward movement letting the river carry them away from this-this terror from the neither world. The old man watched all him friends faint, some were running, he couldn't figure what was wrong.

Inside the chapel devotions stopped, every one jumped and the children looked at their father.

"What was that?" Smenkara asked

"I do not know my son, but we will find out." Pharaoh nodded to a couple of the guards standing by the open balcony, also looking at pharaoh for an answer. The two guards and a couple of priests ran out and around the balcony to the west side of the building.

The sight that confronted them was one of mass confusion and panic. People were coming out of buildings to see what had made such a noise. Looking down the broad main street that ended at the pier, the guards saw a ship in the harbor that was all glowing, but not on fire. And it was moving towards the dock. One of the guards, stunned by what he was looking at, ran back in to Pharaoh. Dropping to his knees, he addressed Pharaoh.

"Great one, there is a strange ship coming into the harbor, it is glowing." Achnaten looked down at his guard. "You mean it is on fire?"

"No great one, it is not on fire, there is a great light on the ship but it is not fire, there is no smoke at all." Pharaoh was interested in this strange ship, there was time before his father the sun would rise. He motioned the guard to rise and pointed to the door. "I would see this strange boat you speak of. The guard stood and led Pharaoh out side. In the distance Pharaoh could see this glowing ship docking. He looked at this strange sight for a few seconds. Not understanding what he was seeing, he told the two guards to go and find out just what this was. And to bring back anyone who could explain just what this was. The two guards bowed and left. On the ship, Mike told the two men he had with him that they would be in front of Isis when they were on shore and lead them to Pharaohs palace. When they were on the pier and ready to make the trip to Pharaohs palace, the two guards noticed an old man standing there just looking around. Sue said "Michael this old man is deaf and has no idea whats happening." Mike looked at the old man and pity hit him. He said to Sue. "Sue, talk to the old man, tell him you are Isis, then give him his hearing back." Sue called the old man to come closer, she spoke to him in his mind. When he realized who his figure was, he fell to his face and started saying a prayer he used to recite before Pharaoh banned the old Gods for his new God. Sue told him to rise and not to be afraid. The old man stood and looking around suddenly hearing what was going on for the first time in many years, tears came to his eye's and again he fell to his knees arms stretched out in front. He couldn't think of the right thing to say, he couldn't thank Isis enough. The one guard, approached the old man and gently moved him to the side. And the two guards, Mike and DJ and Sue, started moving towards Pharaohs palace.

Pharaoh's guards with swords drawn, were heading towards the glowing ship that had docked. But what they were having trouble heading in the direction of the dock, all the people in the small town were running away from the glowing ship. The strange noise had terrorized everyone to the point of insanity. Never had such a noise been heard like that before. Pharaohs guards couldn't believe the scene before them. They tried to stop people but no one could be stopped. Everyone was screaming, everyone was convinced that demons were coming to kill them. The two guards stood to the side letting the people pass. When everyone had passed they started forward, the light from the ship was now on shore and it seemed to be moving closer. Pharaohs men slowly moved in the direction of the light. It was still dark. Some of the merchants had lit torches upon setting up their stands to sell what they could. But those torches gave little light. The light moving towards them was very bright; the two guards shielded their eyes. Then one of them said to the other. "Look, I think I see two figures in front of the light, they look like us, do you see them?" The other man looked closer. "Yes, you are right, come, let's get closer."

Mike and DJ were behind the floating figure of Isis, Sue was sitting and glowing and was floating 18 inches off the ground. "Michael, there are two warriors approaching, they were sent by Pharaoh to find out what is going on." "Okay Sue, how close are they?" "They are almost here Michael, should I stop them." Mike and DJ came from the rear and stood beside the two guards they had placed in front of Sue to lead them to Pharaoh. The two sent by Akanaten were within ten feet of them. They stood with one are covering their eyes because the light was so bright. One of the two men standing with Mike and DJ was looking closer at the two others standing in front of them. He turned to Mike and said. "My lord, I know those two. They were in my command just before Pharaoh took over."

Mike said. "Call to them and identify yourself, tell them to come closer that everything is OK.

Tell them that Isis would speak to them." DJ said to Mike. "Listen, Mike, I think we're going too far with this. If I remember the little bit of Egyptian history we read the other day, the only ancient power to conquer Kemit, was Rome. And at this time in history, Rome isn't even a thought in anyone's mind yet." Mike stopped and thought about what DJ just said.

"You know my friend, your right." Sue broke into their conversation.

"DJ is right Michael; Kemit is in no danger from the Hittites."

"And to be perfectly honest Mike, I'm sick of ancient Egypt."

Mike looked at his friend. "Sue, put everything on hold."

"As you wish Michael." Everything and everyone came to a halt.

Mike walked over to DJ. "You know DJ, I think we could use a good rest, Sue, take us home.

Put everything in this small city back the way it was before we came here today. Bring the people back and wipe all this from their memories. Oh, except one thing." "Yes Michael, I know what you are referring to. It will be done." And in a flash they were back in Mikes house in northern New Jersey. "You know DJ, you were right again. We need a big rest. Sue make us a pizza and a couple of beers. We have a lot to think about."

"You know Mike, what we just did, you know start to change things on a given date in history. And then change our minds and un-do what we did. That opens a door to new adventures. We could go any time in history and do what we want, have fun changing things, and then un-doing It." "That---I don't know how to put it." "Yeah, DJ, I know what you're getting at, and you're Right that does open another door. But I can think of better things to do.

To continue

Printed in the United States
By Bookmasters